Y0-AGI-206

STEPPING
STONES
TO
LOVE

STEPPING STONES TO LOVE

BY

Edith Spacil Gilmore

Philadelphia

THE WESTMINSTER PRESS

LIBRARY OF CONGRESS CATALOG CARD NO. 61-10290

PRINTED IN THE UNITED STATES OF AMERICA

To the Lake Dwellers:

Dear B. and F. and both you A.'s,
L. and Mother B. —
Here's Jane — the girl *has* vexing ways —
Forgive her what you cannot praise
And make her welcome just the same
Because she comes from me.
With love, from E.

Chapter 1

"JANE, what are you lugging away now?" Julian Greene's voice was loud and cross.

With the unwieldy package in her arms and the June sunlight dazzling her eyes, Jane could hardly make out her father's thin, anxious face. From the driver's seat of the little car, he peered up to where she stood on the Greenlands steps, beside one of the white pillars.

"It's a tea set, the one with the little roses. I can carry it, Dad; it doesn't need to go in the car. I put a lot of paper around the cups so they wouldn't break."

"Take it back into the house."

"But, Dad —"

"Take it back into the house, and unpack it and put it where it belongs. When you rent someone a furnished house, you don't make off with the teacups."

"But there are all kinds of cups in the house. I wanted this set because it's the one Mother liked best. I don't want anything to happen to it."

"I'd say there's a lot less chance of things getting damaged with your aunt in charge than with you. The way this place has run down is terrible. I can't imagine what Marion Greene will think when she walks into it tomorrow. Is Rachel at the cottage?"

"Yes — she wanted to fix it up a little for us."

"I'll drive over with this stuff. I'm sure Eleanor Digges wants her car back, and I'll send Rachel here to tidy things up for the Greenes. They're paying her salary now; it isn't right for her to be working for us. Put the china back and come straight to the cottage. I want you to help me unpack my books."

"It's like gatekeepers."

"What?"

"I said, it's like gatekeepers — us living in that little dump all summer and a lot of strangers from New York stampeding all over our house."

"Not strangers, relatives."

"I'll bet they didn't remember they were relatives — and anyhow, distant relatives don't count — till they could get something out of it."

"What can you possibly imagine that they're 'getting out of it'?"

"Oh — this 'Uncle Charles' being president of Halford College when everyone knows you should be."

"I can't stop now to talk about these imaginings of yours, Jane, but they're completely childish and unreal. Sometimes I can't believe you're fifteen!"

He started the engine, and as the car moved off down the broad, winding drive, Jane turned slowly back to the house. The white door with its brass dolphin knocker was ajar; the wide hall that ran all the way through the house was cool and quiet.

Was Greenlands really "run down," as Dad claimed? Jane wondered. He didn't usually notice things very much, and she and Rachel hadn't changed anything from the way Mother used to keep it. She paused in front of the oval mirror with the gilded frame that hung above the drop-leaf table. Her reflection, in the shaded hall, gazed back at her: thin, pale, freckled, wispy-haired — it looked like

8

Dad's face peering from the car! She wedged the tea set under her left arm and traced " Jane Greene " on the table's mahogany surface. Yes, it was dusty — very dusty; her finger tip was black and the letters seemed to stare up at her.

But that wasn't her fault, was it? She had had to go to school after her mother's death, and Rachel, who used to come every day from Maryville and stay all day, had since then come only to do the cooking, because that was all they could afford, Dad claimed. In the fall, when the regular president's house had been fixed up and the new family were living in it, and she and Dad were back here, she would have to learn somehow what to do. It would be really awful if all their beautiful things fell apart because she didn't know how to take care of them! And what about Mother's paintings? Were they all right? Even Dad hadn't objecting to her taking her own picture of the red carnations to the cottage, and he had taken his own painting of the marigolds. But there were lots left — like this little one of lilies of the valley hanging next to the mirror. That had gone all the way to San Francisco for an art show last year! Suppose the pictures got — well, what did happen to pictures? Mildewed, maybe, or warped or something? She would ask Dad; perhaps he would let her come over tonight and take down a few, anyway.

Now for the tea set! She went to the kitchen, pulled open the heavy door from which stairs led down to the stone-floored Greenlands cellars, and clutching the carton carefully to her, made her way to a remote coalbin. There! She couldn't possibly hide a tea set anywhere in the four tiny rooms of the cottage, but it was safe here; the New York Greenes wouldn't be poking around coalbins in the summer.

There wasn't any excuse to stay longer. Or should she

make a last tour? No — because she might cry if she went into the studio upstairs, where Rachel had made a neat pile of the unused canvases and covered them with a cloth. Even going back just one more time to her own room might make her cry. Somebody else would live in it this summer — in her room, with its wide window seat from which she could look right down into the big lilac by the kitchen door and out over the grassy yard to the silver-gray old barn. But maybe no one would want that room; the clotheslines were below that window, and people from New York were very sophisticated and wouldn't like to look at things hung out to dry, or understand what a *safe* feeling it gave her to hear the wet clothes flapping in a strong wind. Probably nobody else ever did feel silly things like that!

About to leave the house, she paused. The drawing room door was open — one last look at that room. The long, low-ceilinged room looked more wonderful than ever, the Oriental rugs glowing softly on the dark, polished floor. But already it didn't seem like home; Rachel had concentrated on getting this room ready for the new people. The marble fireplace had been swept clean of ashes; the low, green-velvet sofa in front of it had no dents in its cushions. Jane was careful not to glance through the French doors at the farther end, because they opened onto the little railed terrace, and beyond it the garden began. From this part of the room, in fact, one could get a glimpse of rose color and white, because the peony bed was in full bloom. " No, we can't possibly come over and look after the garden," Dad had said that morning. " Our tenants are entitled to privacy; they won't want to look out and see us pottering around the grounds! "

Jane turned abruptly and walked out of the house. The door swung shut, softly, heavily; the lock clicked into place with a final sound. It roused Kai from his nap in a patch of shade by one of the fluted pillars; he thumped his tail and rolled one eye sleepily at her.

" Come on, Kai."

He yawned and pretended to fall asleep again.

" Kai, you heard me. Get up and come on. We're going to the cottage. We don't live here any more."

It was nice that Kai was such a big dog; it was comfortable to be able to twist one hand in his collar and feel his warm, shaggy neck as they walked along the narrow footpath that was almost swallowed up by grass and weeds. She was leaving Greenlands for months! Even Dad, who was almost always unreasonable — or, at least, she never knew when he would suddenly be reasonable — couldn't possibly be expecting her to go there at all until the New York Greenes were out of it in the fall.

A fine summer this was going to be! She and Dad would probably get on each other's nerves even more than usual in the tiny cottage. There was not one single person her age left in Halford! If only they could have afforded to go to the lake, like the other faculty families! Not that she had had such a good time there two summers ago when they last went, but there was swimming and a tennis court. Dad had said she could go for a while if any of the girls at school invited her, but nobody had. Now that college was closed, she could get one of the Halford courts without having to wait forever, but with no one to play with except little kids, her game would go to pieces. Ed Marshall, the college coach, had promised to give her lessons this summer. Then Ed had gone to the lake too.

There was the cottage. Seen this way, from the back, how forsaken it looked! Matted ivy left hardly a glimpse of the white brick walls; some tendrils were climbing the sloping roof toward the broad chimney. This part of the Greenlands property was wild and overgrown. Trees and unpruned shrubs crowded close to the little house; a picket fence that had apparently once enclosed it in a square had almost vanished in a tangled mass of green. Kai plunged through the tall grass beside her as she made her way around the house to the front door. Here the car stood at the end of the little rutted drive, small weeds sprouting in the patches where the gravel had washed away.

"Jane — it's about time! All right, Rachel, Jane and I can get the rest of the things in, and you go on back to Greenlands; I'm sure there's plenty to do there still for our tenants. We'll be all right — we'll be, uh, cozy once we've settled in."

"Cozy!" Rachel snorted. "No, Mr. Greene; I don't set foot out of here till I show Janey around a little in the kitchen. Kitchen!" she repeated in a defiant voice, as she and Jane went into the musty, narrow little hall. "Well, here it is." She pushed open the door. "I've been taking a good look at it — call this a kitchen!" Her kind, dark face looked as if she was about to cry.

A rusty gas stove spattered with grease; a refrigerator discolored in yellow patches; plastered walls stained by damp; a copper water boiler by the small sink. Where would they eat? Jane wondered. In here, presumably at the old wooden kitchen table. The two rooms upstairs were bedrooms, and Dad had already said that the only other downstairs room would have to be his study.

"I don't know how you're going to manage here, Janey, honey; it's a shame. I cleaned the refrigerator inside; look, here's some cold beef. You slice some of that for supper for you and your daddy tonight, and here's a jar of scalloped potatoes I made; you heat them up to go with it, but look out they don't burn. This is the way the stove works. It's an awful old thing."

"Look at the fireplace, Rachel. I didn't remember it. I guess all the rooms have them because the cottage is so old — older than Greenlands."

"Fireplace! A fireplace isn't going to be much good to you in a kitchen!" Rachel sat down with a thump in an old rocker that stood beside the fireplace, and glared around her. "I hate to leave you in a lonesome place like this."

"Greenlands doesn't have any houses around it either —"

"But it isn't lonesome," Rachel said firmly. "I'm glad your daddy had the phone put in here at least. You'd better go right on ordering groceries from Hanson's in Maryville the way I've been doing. Only you have to remember to call them before the truck goes out in the morning. They won't deliver afternoons."

"They used to for Mother, all the time, if she forgot something."

Rachel got up hastily and began to arrange a few cans on the shelves of a battered kitchen cupboard. "Anybody would always do anything for Mrs. Greene. Strangers in her house!" she muttered.

"They're — they're relatives, and they're Quakers, like Daddy and me." It was hard trying to cheer up someone if you felt miserable yourself.

"City people! They've been used to living in apartments, most likely — moving every year or two."

"But you don't think they'll do anything awful to the house?"

"They've got two little girls, your daddy said — twins, around five. Children that age are hard on furniture; it's about the worst age. Does your grandmother know about all this?" she asked suddenly.

"Jean? Dad wrote her, but she's in Europe, and she

moves around such a lot it sometimes takes letters a while to catch up."

"There she is, more than enough money to do with — "

"I don't know if she'd give us any now. Daddy hurt her feelings by saying it was against his principles to take any. That was when she wanted to pay for the doctors and everything for Mother."

"Principles," Rachel sighed. "Well, I'll go along to Greenlands now, honey." With a parting hug, she was gone.

In the drawer of the kitchen table were some silverware and a few utensils. Jane cut herself a sliver of the cold beef, and noticed that Rachel had left a box of a dozen eggs. Those would last them quite a while. There was some butter, but only half a loaf of bread. She ought to start keeping a shopping list. But what about laundry — things like sheets and Dad's shirts? Rachel had always done them in the washing machine in the cellar at Greenlands. There was a laundromat in Maryville, but she couldn't very well carry clothes two miles on her bike. Perhaps she could take them on the bus.

"Jane!" Her father appeared in the door. "Come out and help me finish unloading the car. The sooner I can get to work, the better. I'm planning some articles that might bring us in some money, and I want to go over my course notes. I've had to neglect them for the past couple of years, and it isn't fair to my students. Why are you standing there?"

"I was thinking."

"That I doubt. You don't think; you moon around listlessly and never take an interest in anything but tennis." He continued to talk as they carried the cartons from the car into the house. "We'll have to do what we can with this mess today, because tomorrow I want you to go to Greenlands and help your Aunt Marion — or offer to, at least."

" What? Go to Greenlands! "

" Yes, of course. I can't go till late afternoon because I've got a ride to Columbus. I have to look up some things in the library there, and it's a chance to save the bus fare."

" I'm not going to Greenlands at all. Not while it's bursting at the seams with people I've never even seen! "

" I don't know what your not having seen them has to do with it. I've never met Marion myself, and I haven't seen Charles since he was my student here at Halford, twenty years ago."

" Yes, and now he's grabbed the chance to be president — "

" Get that notion out of your head, Jane, if you can. Charles is giving up a brilliant career at Columbia to come here. He's a first-class administrator. The job of president isn't hereditary in our branch of the family, and if it was, I probably couldn't handle it."

" That doesn't make me feel any better about them living in our house — Mother's house — "

" Your mother stayed with them in New York on her way to France, and liked them very much."

" That doesn't have anything to do with it."

" It's pointless to discuss it. But you must go over tomorrow and welcome them. They're our tenants; we're lucky to find any for a house that size. And we're almost the only faculty family left in town. Only Marion and the children are coming for the present, I think. The boy — Peter — must be about your age. Don't drop those journals, Jane, and can't you keep Kai from getting underfoot? "

Kai, surprised and fascinated, was running back and forth with them, his bark of inquiry the only sound in the silence.

" I'll go and see them when they move into the regular president's house."

" Stop a minute, Jane." Dad put down the bulging box

15

he was carrying. " Sit down here on the doorstep. I want to tell you something."

" What? "

" Well — " He sat down beside her and looked at her anxiously. " I'm afraid you'll be pretty upset, but you have to know sooner or later. It's about Greenlands. You seem to take it for granted that we'll be moving back in this fall."

" Take it for granted! Why, of course I do! It's our house, isn't it? Naturally we'll go on living there."

" Jane, when your great-great-grandfather was President of Halford and built Greenlands, labor was cheap and servants too, and he built on a grand scale. The official president's house was put up a lot later — I think when one of the Diggeses was president about 1910 — and it's not nearly so well constructed. In fact, it's pretty dilapidated right now, and the elm that fell on the roof has just about finished it."

" The trustees are going to fix it up. You told me so."

" They aren't so sure now. They had an estimate made, and some of them feel the repairs wouldn't be worth it. They may want that land for a new dormitory. If I sold them Greenlands to use as the president's house, Charles and Marion could afford to run it. The salary is quite good, and Marion has considerable money of her own, I think."

" Sell Greenlands! "

" Don't make yourself miserable about it yet. Perhaps I shouldn't have mentioned it, because the whole idea could still fall through. The trustees might change their minds again, or perhaps they won't offer me enough to make it worth-while selling the place."

" I can't stand the idea."

" But, Jane, with the way our finances stand, I don't believe we could keep Rachel even part time. How can you go to school and keep house too? "

16

"I'll learn — somehow. I'll earn some money too. Oh, Dad — "

"There's another thing. I've never considered Greenlands really suitable for a Quaker family. Especially not if it means struggling along in debt. But cheer up, pup, we'll see." He patted her shoulder, picked up his box, and went into the house.

That was just like Dad. Thinking that patting her shoulder and calling her "pup" was enough to make her feel better about the most awful thing that had happened to her since Mother died!

Kai's head was in her lap; she lifted it gently by the ears and looked into his eyes. "Oh, Kai!" He plunged up to lick her ear, and she put her arms around him. "I suppose you're wondering why we don't go home to Greenlands now, aren't you? Oh, Kai."

Chapter II

Now that the back door of Greenlands was in sight, it would be safer, Jane decided, to get off her bicycle before someone heard the sound of it on the gravel path. She wheeled it carefully toward the wide kitchen stoop. "Sh-h, Kai."

This was the time to follow out her plan, to turn right around and go back to the cottage. When Dad got back from Columbus, she could say: "I did go to Greenlands. I went right up to the door. But I couldn't go in. I just couldn't! My heart failed me!" That would impress him.

How quiet it was, not a sound! Perhaps the New York family hadn't come yet. But Rachel must be here; she had planned to take the seven-thirty bus from Maryville.

The kitchen door swung open suddenly. "Kai!" Her

grab at his collar was too late. He bounded forward into the kitchen, and a boy's voice said, " Hi, dog! "

Jane jumped on her bike so quickly that the wheels slued around in the gravel and it toppled over, carrying her with it. Before she could untangle herself, a tall boy came out of the house and stood looking down at her.

" Are you O.K.? " He reached down and lifted the bike and pulled her to her feet.

" Of course I am." How asinine! Jane thought. What an idiotic thing to do — like some kid, learning to ride a bicycle! The pedal had scraped her shin, too, right through her jeans. It hurt so much she could feel her eyes watering, and hoped the boy didn't notice.

" Your bike looks all right." He smiled at her as she took the handle bars. " My name's Pete Greene."

" I — I know." Jane felt hot and embarrassed. What a sensationally good-looking boy he was, with his gray eyes and thick, dark lashes and his crew cut! And Kai, who usually wouldn't have anything to do with strangers, was making up to him — someone he'd never seen before.

" You're from the Halford drugstore, aren't you? " Pete looked at the closed wicker bike basket she used for schoolbooks. " They told my mother on the phone they'd send somebody over with the things she wanted. But she isn't here now; she took the cleaning lady and my kid sisters to — where is it, Maryville? — to get some groceries."

" No, I'm not from the drugstore. I guess I'd better be going. I mean, I have a lot of stuff to do. Kai, come on! "

" What's your hurry? Sit down, why don't you, and give me the low-down on this place? " He sat down himself and stretched comfortably. " It's the living end, seems to me — or maybe dead end is more like it." He looked around him at the yard and the clothesline and over at the barn. " What's your name? "

"Jane Greene."

"Oh, cut it out! I've got some kind of distant cousin here named Greene."

"Yes — I mean, I'm your distant cousin."

He sat up with a jerk. "Mother said about my age. I'm sixteen and a half."

"I'm going on sixteen myself." Pete looked surprised, Jane saw. Everyone always said she looked about twelve.

"Isn't your name supposed to be Jessica?" he asked.

"It is — legally, I guess. I was named for my mother. But my middle name is Jane, and that's what I want to be called. I decided that years ago."

"O.K.," Pete laughed. "Hi, Cousin Jane! Why are you standing around as if you're going to take off any minute? Sit down and relax. I know — wait a second." He went into the kitchen and came back with a round tin box. "These are some cookies we brought along to eat in the car, but we didn't polish them all off. Let's have some. The hound too, if he likes cookies. What's *his* name?"

"We call him Kai."

"Nice dog. Here, Jane, try one of these with the gold paper around them; they're made of almonds."

Jane unwrapped the cooky. It looked delicious, and so did the chocolate one Pete was munching and the one with slivers of red cherry on it that he gave to Kai. Not that Kai ought to be hungry. He had eaten up the burned scrambled eggs she had made for the first cottage breakfast. Scrambling eggs looked so easy when Rachel did it! Perhaps they had better have cold cereal and milk in the mornings.

"Why didn't your dad come over with you?" Pete asked. "Mother wants to meet him."

"He asked me to say he was sorry, but he had to go to Columbus today to the library, and he'll stop by here on his way back. He said for me to ask your mother if I could do anything. Like — like showing her the house and where things are or anything like that. But Rachel knows, of course. She can show her as well as I could, or better, probably, lots better! " She felt a sudden pang; if only she could get away — just get up and go away from Greenlands and this boy lounging on the step as if he owned the place! There was nothing to stop her, but then her father would make her come over again. If she could say she had done something at least, it might save some of the fuss and argument when he got back from Columbus. " I know what, Pete — we could walk in to Halford. It's only half a mile and a pretty road, and I could show you around."

Pete stretched out his long legs and leaned back. The sun was on his face, and his white shirt, open at the neck, looked dazzling against his tanned skin. " I guess everything in the house is pretty well under control. Or it will be in no time. Mother's a dynamo, and she likes to get her teeth into something new and organize things. As for Halford, we drove through it when we came this morning — so we've seen it, haven't we? What's there to show me? College buildings, a little bunch of houses, drugstore, gas station, post office, and that's it. You've had it."

" Well, I know Halford isn't one of the big colleges — "

" It sure isn't."

" But you knew that before you came. Your father must have told you all about it lots of times."

" I don't know about ' lots of times.' He's mentioned it. After all, he went to college here himself."

" What's so peculiar about that? "

" Wait a minute. I didn't say it was peculiar — not exactly."

" You sounded as if you thought it was peculiar. You'll be going to college here yourself. All the Greenes have, even the New York ones, ever since our ancestor founded it."

20

"I know. All the Greenes have — and the time has now come to stop. I want a lot better science course than you can get here unless my old man builds a fire under the place and stirs things up a little. He says the only really good department here is history."

"That's what my father teaches."

"I know. He must be pretty old, isn't he, if my pop was his student?"

"He is pretty old; he's about fifty."

"Another thing — even if I could get the kind of courses I want here, I wouldn't go to a Quaker college. I kicked like a steer when Dad said he was going to take this job."

"You mean you didn't *want* your father to be president of Halford?"

"Do you think I've got rocks in my head? I go to Andover, and I like living in New York. That's where most of the guys I hang out with at school live too."

"I thought you probably went to one of the big Quaker places — like Westtown, maybe. I got their catalog once."

"Thanks a lot — but no, thanks! Where do you go?"

"Right here at Halford School. It's just a little school that the faculty kids go to. We have some of our own teachers, and a few of the college professors teach too. Except for the college, there are all farms around here. Most of the farm kids go in to the central high school in Maryville, but if their families are Quakers, they come to Halford School."

"I can picture the whole setup!" said Pete. "Everything strict, real Bible-belt stuff, isn't it? I bet you can't smoke at the college."

"Not on campus."

"I knew it. That's exactly the kind of rule that would make me want to start smoking. Do the school and the college have regular dancing?"

"Oh, yes, they do now! The college has proms in the gym — that's where there's a movie once a week too. And there's a lot of square dancing and folk dancing. And — there are the college tennis tournaments every fall."

" I'll take New York. Or at least, I would if I could. Is there anyone around this summer who's our age, Jane, except us? "

" All the faculty families are away. Most of them have cottages at Linden Lake, and that's pretty far. Mary Lee Stebbins'll be back soon, and you'll meet her, all right! She went to a Young Friends Conference, but I think it was only to meet boys."

" That sounds reasonable. What's she like? "

" Oh, never mind now, Pete. I want to know what you meant about your father and Halford. You were kidding, weren't you, when you said that? About not wanting him to be president? Because if you really don't like the idea — "

" I don't, I tell you. I don't think my mother does, either. Why would she like it? She's got a part-time job in New York she's mad about — she's a psychologist — and all her relatives live there or on Long Island, a whole raft of cousins and aunts. They're a lot of fun, most of them. And my kid sisters go to a kindergarten they think is just fine. It's very progressive; they teach them to be demons there."

" Then maybe you won't be staying long, Pete! Do you think so? I heard my father say that your father wouldn't promise to come for more than a year — "

" Thanks! "

" Oh — " Her voice must have sounded awfully eager. " Look — I didn't mean it that way exactly — "

" So what did you mean? "

It was a reasonable question for Pete to ask, but how could she possibly explain anything so private and embarrassing to a stranger? If Pete's father did leave Halford after a year, Dad would most likely become President. He had said once that the trustees had considered him for it very seriously. It would make such a difference — all the difference in the world! Dad would be happier, not so hard to get along with, and there would be more money. Enough, maybe, to pay what they owed and to have Rachel back all the time, and even old Lonnie, Rachel's uncle, to be gardener, the way he had always been. Dad had hated having to tell Lonnie they couldn't afford him any more.

" Wake up! " said Pete.

" I was thinking — about what I said, I mean. I know it isn't your fault that you've moved to Halford — "

" My fault! "

" Well, it's too hard to explain."

" My fault — Listen! Do you know where I was this last summer? " He glared around him. " Grindelwald, that's where I was! "

" What's Grindelwald? "

" Swiss village, smack in the Alps, sensational climbing! We spend almost every summer in Europe."

" You aren't the only person who ever went abroad! "

" What? "

" I said you aren't the only person who ever went to Europe! Jean practically lives there; she doesn't think a thing about it; she goes back and forth all the time and lives in Paris or somewhere for a while. She shuts up the apartment in Columbus — it's huge — "

" Wait! " said Pete. " What are you all excited about? You've left me 'way behind; I don't even know who Jean is! "

" She's my grandmother on my mother's side." Pete was looking amazed. It had been silly to flare up like that. " She's not much older than Dad. That's young for a grand-mother, and she looks younger, anyway, so I call her Jean.

She likes it. I could go to Europe with her any time, only I haven't happened to feel like it. She's always inviting me! "

That was perfectly true; Jean did always invite her. The fact that Dad wouldn't ever let her go, and didn't even like to have her go to Columbus to stay with Jean when she was home, was something private that a person naturally wouldn't tell a stranger. So it wasn't like telling lies.

" I still don't know why you're all worked up about it," said Pete, "but let's skip it." He got up. " Come on in and show me around the house. It's so big I haven't seen it all."

" Oh, Pete! "

" Now what? "

" I don't want to — I can't! " Pete was looking very surprised again; by now he must think she was feeble-minded or something. " Look, let's go to Halford, the way I said, and I'll show you the president's house. That's the one you'll be living in, where the tree fell in on the roof — "

" Is that what's eating you? Is that what all this is about — us being in your house? "

" I guess so. Anyway I — I haven't got used to the idea yet."

" It probably should have occurred to me. But look, Jane, aren't you taking it out on me? Why do that? I didn't have any part in it, and I don't care where I live if I have to be away from the places I like. After all, your father wanted to rent it."

" I know he did."

" What a production! " But his voice didn't sound really cross. " Can't you snap out of it? After all, you can come here any time you feel like it."

" That isn't the same thing."

" I know it isn't — but what else can I say? Why all this fuss about a house? It's nice, and I think all that old furniture is great, but we aren't going to hurt it. Why so much excitement?"

"It's — it's partly because of my mother. She liked the house so much — especially the garden."

"That is rough." Pete's voice was gentle. "I guess you miss her a lot. She was sick quite a long time, wasn't she? I remember her; she stayed at our house a few days that time she went to France. Everyone thought she was wonderful."

"Most people's mothers don't go abroad by themselves, I guess — not to stay for a long time, anyway. But my mother was a well-known artist."

"I know. We've got one of her pictures in New York in our living room, and sometimes an art gallery asks to borrow it. The reason my dad's not here is that he's doing some research in Provence for a book he's writing, and then going to an education conference in London afterward. I know how you feel, more or less. He and I get pretty sore at each other sometimes, but he's really a good guy. I was going to go with him, and then a whole lot of stuff came up and I couldn't."

"But, Pete, having someone be away for a while — that's not the same as — as having someone die!"

"I didn't say it was."

"If that's all the problem you have — having your father go away for a little while, and having to live in a place that you don't know anything about yet, but you've made up your mind you don't like because it isn't as big as New York — "

"Hey, stop! I never did say that was all the problems I have. Why do you want to bicker all the time?"

"I wasn't bickering!"

"Yes, you were. You may not know it, but you were. Do you always go around fighting with people like this?"

25

"Hi, Jane!" Billy Baker shot around the corner of the house on his bicycle and brought it to a stop, his round, blue eyes fixed curiously on Pete. "I'm from the drugstore; my grandfather sent me over with some stuff, but nobody answered the front door." He handed Pete a white parcel.

"This is Billy Baker from Halford, Pete. His grandfather is Clerk of Halford Meeting." What a nice little boy Billy was, with his broad, cheerful grin! It was just as well he'd turned up before she and Pete had a fight. Why was it that people couldn't seem to understand the most simple things about her sometimes? Like the way she felt about the house, for instance. Didn't Pete know that Greenlands was famous because it was so beautiful? People came and took pictures of it for magazines.

"I guess your pop's the new president, huh?" Billy was asking Pete. "Big deal! Hey, Jane — did you get a chance yet to ask about you-know-what?"

"Not yet, but I will, and I'll call you, Billy. We've got a telephone at the cottage."

"I bet it seems peculiar, living there. I'll come and see you. Don't forget about my tennis lesson, Jane — and don't forget to ask about — " He nodded in Pete's direction, got on his bicycle, and rode off, whistling.

"Ask about what?" Pete inquired.

"Oh — " It was rather embarrassing to bring it up now. "It was only something I was going to have my father ask your mother about. There's a pond called Stepping Stones, not very big, that belongs to Greenlands; it's in the woods. It's about the only place near Halford to swim, and there are some little kids around this summer, like Billy and Mary Lee's brothers and sisters. Their mother'll let them swim if I go too. I promised Billy I'd find out if we could go there sometimes this summer."

"I don't get it."

" Will your mother let us? "

" Why wouldn't she let you? "

" This isn't my house this summer — " and perhaps not ever again. " If it isn't my house, then naturally it isn't my pond — "

" Oh, cut it out. That's all an act if I ever heard one. You don't seem to have a lot of sense, but if you've got enough to get by with, why should you think that my mother would be mean about a thing like that? You can live in the pond like a frog if you want to — and Billy too, and anyone else who feels like it. Asking about it the way you did is only a way to make me feel like a heel. Poor little martyred Jane, bounced out of the old homestead! "

Jane picked up her bicycle. " Come on, Kai, I guess we won't hang around here any more."

" So long, Cousin Jane. It's been really real," Pete called after her, and it sounded as if he was laughing.

Chapter III

Oh, Dad! Supper isn't ready yet. I — didn't know when to expect you from Columbus."

" It doesn't matter; I'm not hungry." He sat down in the rocker and put his brief case on the floor.

How tired and discouraged he looked, Jane thought — and how awful the kitchen looked, with the breakfast dishes not done, and Kai gnawing an old bone under the sink.

" I didn't get around to calling Hanson's this morning, Dad, and then I thought I'd bike in to Maryville this afternoon and buy some stuff to eat — " But she hadn't; she had made herself a sandwich of the last of the cold beef

27

when she came back to the cottage after the talk with Pete, and had spent the rest of the afternoon at Stepping Stones.

" Anything we have'll do, Jane. But you must learn to keep us in supplies."

" It — it was partly because I went to Greenlands this morning that I forgot about groceries. You said I had to go, and I went, but I didn't go in the house. I met Pete and he asked me to, but my heart failed me."

" Yes, mine almost did too."

" What! "

" I've just come from there. I went over on my way back from town, but to tell you the truth, pup, I didn't enjoy waiting at the front door to be let in."

" Of course you didn't, Dad! "

" I did go in, as you'll have to, sooner or later, and had a cup of coffee with your Aunt Marion and saw the children."

" If you minded, Dad, more than you thought you would, does that mean you'll really try hard to keep the house? Does it? I'll do anything in the world I can to help keep it! Dad, think of the garden, Mother's garden, going to rack and ruin already — "

" Gardens don't go to rack and ruin overnight; after all, we were pruning the rhododendrons only yesterday morning."

" Lonnie always said you must never let a garden slip back, not even a week, if you — if you love it. But, Dad, about keeping Greenlands — "

" Well — " he began slowly, " I want to talk about it with you. Wait! Isn't that a car out front? "

" Oh! "

" Can't be helped; we'll have to discuss it later."

The front door opened. " Anybody home? " called

28

Eleanor Digges's voice. She came along the hall and into the kitchen without waiting for an answer, beaming through her glasses, her round face shiny as usual. Dad had said once when Jane had criticized Eleanor's looks, " For a girl who never wears anything but jeans and a ragged T shirt if she can help it — " But there wasn't any point in her dressing up. Not that there was much really for Eleanor, either, because she wasn't interesting-looking at all. And she always picked clothes that made her look even plumper than she was, like the blue cotton dress with a wide white belt she was wearing now.

" Good evening, Julian! How is thee, Janey, dear? Now this isn't a call — not a real call — " But she sat down all the same. " I wouldn't pay a call when anybody's just moved and everything's upset. But my strawberry plants have done so marvelously this year, and I couldn't resist making a cake, though I know I shouldn't eat whipped cream! Then I thought, I'll never finish it up by myself, so I'll run over and see how things are at the cottage and if there's anything I can do, and take Julian and Janey some of the cake for a dessert."

" That's very nice of thee, Eleanor. After all, thee's not exactly a visitor, thee knows! " Dad sounded pleased, Jane thought. If he encouraged Eleanor, she would be hanging around the cottage all the time! Using plain speech when he talked with her made it seem more as if she was actually a relative. Maybe Mother's not having been a birthright Friend was the reason they had never used plain speech much at Greenlands. Of course, Dad had known Eleanor all his life; she was always telling that story of how when she was a little girl she got lost in the woods near Stepping Stones after a picnic. The men and older boys looked for her, and it was Dad who found her eventually, asleep under a bush or something. That was all there was to the story. But Eleanor thought anything about Halford or Halford people was interesting. That was one of the things that made her so boring!

" I'll go ahead with getting supper, Eleanor," Jane said.

" Certainly, honey! "

It was hard, Jane thought, as she collected the unwashed breakfast dishes, to do something you weren't used to doing in a place you weren't used to, if there was someone watching you. She looked in the refrigerator to see what might be left of the last Greenlands supplies Rachel had brought over. Three frankfurters. That should be easy — frankfurters and canned beans. Was there any catchup? Eleanor, obviously, was only half listening to what Dad was telling her about what he'd been reading in Columbus — she was just itching to take over and help. Because Eleanor had been Mother's friend, she seemed to think she owned the whole family and that Jane couldn't do anything for herself. How maddening to have her go on sitting there when Dad had been about to talk about Greenlands and keeping Greenlands! How long would she stay? What a job it was to open a can with a rusty opener like this one!

Kai got up and brought his awful old bone over to Dad and Eleanor. He liked to be near people, especially if they were talking, but Dad was now looking closely at the bone and then around the room in general, and he sighed. " I'll tell thee who's moved without any muddle, Eleanor, and that's Marion Greene. I've been over at Greenlands. I thought I ought to stop by, her first day there."

" Julian, how exciting! I'd forgotten; I thought they weren't due till tomorrow! I remember Charles as a student, of course, but he's abroad, isn't he? What is his wife like? "

" Marion seems to be a nice, sensible woman — no

beauty, considering how good-looking all the children are."

" Now, let me see; there's a boy about Janey's age."

" That's right. Pete. Looks a lot like Charles and has very good manners. The two girls are twins, almost six."

" Then I'll have them in my first grade this fall, I suppose, said Eleanor. " Lambs! "

" They were playing Indians in the shrubbery," said Dad, "but I suppose they are lambs."

That sounded a little sarcastic, but Eleanor never noticed when people were sarcastic. Wasn't she ever going? She was carefully not looking at the table, which looked almost as bad set for supper as it did with the dirty breakfast dishes on it. There was a tablecloth from Greenlands somewhere in one of the cartons in the hall; Rachel had put it in without telling Dad. Was heating up a can of beans all there was to it? Didn't Rachel put in molasses or something? Dad's tea must be steeped enough by now, but there didn't seem to be a strainer anywhere around. She probably shouldn't have started it before starting to broil the frankfurters.

" Janey! " Eleanor was practically breathing down the back of her neck. " I'm so afraid thee'll hurt thyself if thee tries to light the broiler like that. Look, I think the match goes here, through this little hole — "

" For heaven's sake, Jane, are you trying to blow us up? Here, let me do it."

" I don't want the broiler at all. I'm going to boil the franks."

" All right, Janey dear. I didn't mean to interfere — I know it's hard to get used to a new kitchen. I'll run along now, and thee can bring me back the basket any time thee's in Halford."

But, being Eleanor, she went on chattering all the time

31

Dad walked out to her car with her, and probably after she'd gotten into it. At least the franks were boiling by the time Dad came back. Was it worth taking the bread out of its wrapper?

" Jane —"

" Oh, O.K., Dad; I'm sorry."

" It's lucky Eleanor doesn't take offense easily."

" I said I'm sorry! Please, Dad, sit down and eat — it's all ready — and tell me what you think about Greenlands."

" Our silent grace first, Jane."

Jane bowed her head and thought how quiet the cottage was, now that Eleanor's chirping voice was gone. The trees that crowded close to it were motionless; the occasional thump of Kai's tail seemed almost to shake the floor.

" Let's suppose," said Dad, as he began to eat, " that I'm able to make some arrangement with the bank and we do move back into Greenlands — what about the house-keeping? We wouldn't be able to afford any help to speak of, and I can't help much. There's not only the work on my courses, but also the articles I want to work on. I used to sell some now and then to magazines and newspapers, on contemporary events from a historian's point of view. It's valuable to me professionally to publish that kind of thing, and that's our only hope of additional income."

" I'll learn to cook and dust and everything, Dad! There isn't so much to it, is there? I'll get Eleanor to teach me. She'll like it, and I don't really have anything against her. I can stand her perfectly well if I have to."

" What about your schoolwork, though? You'll have to do better this year —"

" I didn't flunk anything but algebra, Dad."

" That's not good enough."

" I'll study more, and I'll work a little bit on the algebra every day this summer, for the make-up exam. And listen,

32

Dad; I've just had a sensational idea about money! Someone used to live in this cottage. There was some furniture here."

"Yes. One year when you were a baby we let a couple of senior boys from the college live in it rent free because they were hard up. They looked after the Greenlands furnace for me and did some other odd jobs. They left some furnishings, and some were here to begin with."

"Suppose Eleanor could show me how to fix it up? I could splash some paint around and make it look nice enough so we could rent it in the fall. There're always some new young faculty couples looking for places to live."

"Maybe." Dad looked around him doubtfully. "It's a solid enough little place, as far as construction goes. There's even a little furnace in the cellar. But I can't give you much of any cash for your renovation schemes, Jane."

"I know I can at least make the yard look a lot nicer without having to spend much money. I saw some garden tools in the cellar when I came over here the other day. They're rusty, but I'll clean them — " She stopped, for she could tell from her father's sad expression that he was thinking about the Greenlands garden. "Dad, Rachel asked me if Jean knew about us having to move here."

"Yes, I wrote her, and the letter's probably caught up with her by now. She'll be sorry; she likes Greenlands. It was one of the few things — " and he stopped short. Jane knew what he had started to say: "that reconciled her to having your mother marry me!" Did Dad think she wasn't bright enough to know how Jean felt? "Well, it's too late now," he went on, "for any help from there, even if I was willing to accept it. But there's another possibility we've never talked about, Jane, and that's the pictures."

"You mean, sell Mother's paintings?"

"They were starting to bring good prices when she became ill. All the ones at Greenlands are ours to do as we like with them."

" Oh, Dad — "

" It wouldn't seem like home without them, would it? "

" If — if they were gone, it would be harder to — to remember her."

" I know. Besides, I feel they ought to stay together as a collection, and that wouldn't be easy, to sell them all together."

" I've been worrying about them — if they're safe, I mean, Dad."

" They're much safer at Greenlands than in a damp-feeling little house like this, and I'm sure your aunt will look after things properly."

" City people live in apartments, and move every couple of years, and don't know how to appreciate old houses."

" Now that's an absurd, arbitrary judgment, Jane."

" I don't even know what ' arbitrary ' means, exactly."

" In the way I've just used it, it means you've made a judgment that isn't based either on logic or full information. Marion was enthusiastic about Greenlands, but kept wanting to know if we'd taken enough things from there to make us comfortable, and when we'd come there for a meal. We must be careful not to accept more favors from her than we can repay."

" I don't want to accept any at all. Or from Pete, either. I didn't like him."

" Nonsense. You don't know him well enough to dislike him. In any case, you'd better make up your mind to seeing a good deal of him. Marion was rather upset to discover how few young people there are in Halford this summer, and apparently feels that for some reason it's better for Pete to be here than with his father. You'll meet Marion after Meeting for Worship tomorrow."

" Dad — "

" Jane, let's not have another argument about your going to Meeting."

" All right — if I have to."

" You do have to." He pushed aside his plate with some beans still on it, and looked hungrily at Eleanor's dessert, a creamy-white and scarlet mound.

" I'll cut the cake, Dad, but I guess I'd better heat up your tea — or make some more. I let it get too strong."

" Oh, I'll drink it as it is," but he looked sadly at the dark-brown stream pouring into his cup.

" I didn't know there was anything hard about cooking beans and franks. It'll probably take me quite a while to learn to cook anything fancy."

" It's not that I mind beans, Jane — "

" These got a little bit burned, I guess. But you always say Quakers should live simply so they can give money away to — to orphans or something."

" That's right; they should. But an unburned baked bean is simple enough for me."

" I'll learn. I'll learn anything — anything in the world, if it's for Greenlands."

" Well, I hope it is, pup. We'll try."

" I'll learn to cook. I'll learn to clean. I'll learn how to iron your shirts. I'll study my horrible algebra. I promise."

" I won't promise anything, because I don't quite see my way clear to fulfilling any rash guarantees I might make."

" Promise to try Dad. Promise to keep the house if you can."

" That's safe enough. I want Greenlands too. We'll keep it if we possibly can. I promise."

Chapter IV

How absolutely endless Meeting for Worship seemed this morning! thought Jane. If only the Meetinghouse clock was up front, but it wasn't. If she twisted her head around to see what time it was, Dad wouldn't like it. Marion Greene and Pete, if he was with his mother, must have come to Meeting after them and be sitting somewhere behind. It must be twelve o'clock by now. It could be even later.

Some people thought old Wilbur Baker wasn't the best person to be Clerk of the Meeting, because often during Meeting he meditated so deeply that he forgot to notice the time and didn't give the signal for Meeting to end by shaking hands with whoever was next to him on the Facing Bench. Anyone who was sitting next to Wilbur Baker respected him too much to do anything about it, like jogging his elbow, or coughing very loudly. Nobody had spoken very much in Meeting today, and that made it seem longer.

It was weird to think that not so very long ago she had liked going to Meeting so much that she never could decide which she liked better — a Meeting that was mostly silence, or one in which a lot of people got up and talked.

Eleanor Digges, sitting on the bench just across the aisle from them, shifted a little, then clutched suddenly at her purse as it slid from her lap. It was typical of her to miss it, and the noise it made sounded like a crash in the quiet of the Meetinghouse, but Wilbur Baker had his eyes closed and did not stir.

Meetings for Worship used to last two or three hours sometimes. But that was a long time ago, hundreds of years back, when the Quakers began and her ancestor Jonas Greene got converted. Had Pete looked at the little picture of Jonas in the Greenlands library? It was a woodcut from a book of memoirs. Jonas looked pretty grim in the picture, and he was wearing a hat like a beehive. It was all right for Pete to make cracks about martyrs, and having to leave the old family homestead, but it *was* like a story, a family that had to leave its home and its ancestral portraits. Only Jonas was Pete's ancestor too, so that was a little different.

If Meeting was going to go on and on forever, it would be a good idea to try to think about something nice. It wasn't any use to brood about the New York Greenes being in her house, or about how Dad had forced her to come to Meeting this morning — like a slave or something. Or about having to meet Marion Green after Meeting. Or about tennis, and how Ed Marshall hadn't kept his promise to coach her this summer, and was probably giving lessons to the Halford School kids at the lake every day. She would say the longest poem she knew by heart over to herself — " The Forsaken Merman " — because it was so cool-sounding and she could imagine what the sea was like, long, rolling swells of jade green. Or she would think about going back to Greenlands in the fall, and, first of all, running out into the garden . . .

At last Wilbur Baker was shaking hands with Lancaster Seaman, and everybody else was stirring and shaking hands too, and starting to get up and go out.

" All right, Jane, come along, now." Dad towed her down the aisle as if she didn't have enough sense to get out the door by herself.

"Everyone who's here will be wanting to meet Marion, but we'll say hello. She's over there."

Jane saw Pete too, standing by his mother on the Meetinghouse lawn, under the big sycamore. He was taller than his mother, and it was hard to see her because a lot of the people who had been in Meeting were already milling around them, all wanting to get a look at the new president's family. Maybe some of them had come just to see the New York Greenes.

Perhaps Dad would say they'd better go back to the cottage and another time would do — No, no such luck! Marion Greene had somehow detached herself from the crowd and was coming toward them, a woman with a large nose and mouth and a somewhat stocky figure. But her dress, Jane decided, was lovely — some kind of gray, silky-looking jersey, very cool and simple, and around her neck she was wearing a double row of some wonderful lavender-colored stones. Could those be amethysts?

"Julian, good morning! How nice to see you again — and what a little gem of a Meetinghouse! I love it! And this is Jane!" Her handclasp was nice and firm, not damp or flabby, and Jane sniffed cautiously to take in a wonderful smell, spicy and cool and clean. It must be some very expensive perfume. "Jane, dear, I've been looking forward to meeting you ever since I knew we were coming to Halford. You don't know how often I've tried to picture what you were like — a grown-up niece that I'd never even laid eyes on!"

"How do you do, Marion Greene." It was necessary to be very polite with Dad right there, watching her like a hawk. But "niece" was going a little bit too fast — for a distant relative by marriage! Anyhow, Pete's mother ought to be feeling a little apologetic at least about being in Greenlands! Jane's calling her "Marion Greene" was like saying " Mrs. Greene " among people who weren't Quakers. It was perfectly polite — nobody could claim it wasn't — but it would show that Jane wasn't ready to make friends with a total newcomer. Sincere people who meant what they said didn't start gushing the minute they met a person.

" Pete told me you like to be called Jane rather than Jessica. You and I must have a long talk about your beautiful mother someday. We loved her visit to us. I've never met anyone who had so much vitality and talent — as well as being so lovely to look at! We always brag about being related to her, to our artist friends. Your father says the little house you're in is quite close to Greenlands. I'm glad; that means we'll see a lot of you, doesn't it? Now I must go and talk to some of these people. But when can you come over and really get acquainted? "

" Well, I — I'm pretty busy — "

" That's silly, Jane," said Dad. " I'll come and introduce some of the Friends to you, Marion. As to Jane being busy — "

People started to swarm around Marion Greene again. It was too bad, Jane thought, that Dad got cut off from her too, because now Pete came strolling over, and it was going to be harder to talk to him with Dad standing right there.

" Good morning, Uncle Julian. Hi, Jane! "

" Hi, Pete! " Whatever Pete was like as a person, it was somehow upsetting to look at him, standing there smiling at them. The sun glinted on his teeth, which were very strong and white and even, and on his short, smoky-black hair. Yes, he looked like the picture, in her old book of Grimm's fairy tales, of the youngest of the seven princes who got turned into swans. The picture showed him leaning against a marble fountain, his left arm a swan's wing, the way it always would be. The princes' sister never did get time to finish the last of the seven shirts woven of nettles, which broke the spell.

"Can't we give you and Jane a lift home, sir? That's our car, over there." Pete nodded at a big, new-looking convertible standing at the curb. "I had to talk Mother and Dad into getting it. They don't think it looks like a Quaker family car, but we compromised. I wanted a Jaguar; we settled for this, and now that we have it, they like it. It's fine with the top down, and the twins are crazy about it."

"I suppose you left them at the First Day School?"

"Yes, sir. They've probably demolished it by now."

"Janey!" Eleanor Digges came trotting up to them. "Good morning, Julian. And don't thee tell me, Julian, who this nice young man is, because I can guess. Thee must be Charles Greene's boy, Peter." She shook hands. "How's thee do, dear? I'm Eleanor Digges."

"How's thee do, Eleanor Digges," said Pete.

"I teach first grade at Halford School," Eleanor rattled on, "and I'm an old friend of Janey's. But, then, the Diggeses and the Greenes have always known each other, ever since Halford was founded. Thy father must have told thee about it, and of course I knew him when he came here to college. That's thy mother, isn't it, talking to Wilbur Baker — that old gentleman in plain clothes? I won't wait to meet her now, but thee tell her, Peter, when thee gets a chance, that I'm going to pop in on her at Greenlands this afternoon, to see if I can do anything for her. I know Greenlands very well, thee sees, because I was dear Jessica Greene's closest friend here in Halford."

Didn't Eleanor mind at all, Jane wondered, seeing someone else in Mother's house? Apparently not, or she wouldn't be going there of her own accord, and so much as a matter of course! Mother had always been so wonderful to Eleanor, teasing her and laughing at some things about her, like the way she fussed over housekeeping, and thought that everything that happened in the Meeting or in Halford was so important, but never in a way that hurt Eleanor's feelings. When Eleanor had tried to speak at the Memorial Meeting that was held after Mother had died, she had ended up by crying, right there in Meeting.

"Janey, I was wondering — if thee's got something all planned for dinner at the cottage, I won't say another word. But if thee hasn't, or if it's something that will keep just as well as not — well, I put a little roasting chicken in my oven before I came to Meeting, and hoped Wilbur wouldn't keep us till it was overdone. It ought to be done right now, nice and brown, and more than enough for the three of us. What does thee say, dear? And thee, Julian?"

"You go, Dad, why don't you?" Jane urged, remembering that she had not ordered any groceries yesterday.

"I'm having candied sweet potatoes too, Janey!"

"I can't, Eleanor. I shut up Kai so he wouldn't follow us, and I have to go and let him out and feed him."

"Now, Jane, that can wait!" Dad said, and they both began to try to argue her into going. Luckily Wilbur Baker came along, with his lovely, clean white beard looking like silver in the sun, and when Dad started to tell him about it, he took Jane's side.

"When thee was Jane's age, Julian," Wilbur Baker said, "thee was every bit as stubborn as she is, and there's many a time I don't think thee's altogether outgrown it yet. The best thing, usually, was to let thee have thy own way; thee often found thee didn't like it so well, after all. Thee go along with Eleanor now, and let Jane do as she likes."

After Dad and Eleanor had started off, down Meeting-house Street, Wilbur Baker shook hands with Pete and looked at him carefully. "Well, Peter Greene! It's a good day for Halford when the Greenes come back where they belong."

"Wilbur Baker, Pete says he doesn't want to go to college here. He doesn't want to go to Halford School for his senior year, either; he's going back to Andover."

" So? " said Wilbur Baker, and looked at Pete again from under his thick white eyebrows. " We'll see. It isn't always easy to leave Halford, as thy father once found, Jane."

" Dad? "

" Well, thee knows he worked for the Service Committee in the Tirol when he wasn't much older than Peter here."

" Most Quakers do something like that for a year or two, sir, don't they? " Pete asked.

" Julian Greene wanted to stay. He wanted to live in the mountains. Didn't thee know that, Jane? But he came back." Then, changing his voice, and making it rumbly, he said suddenly, " Has thee got a pain, Jane? "

" No, Wilbur Baker."

" Then what's the good of my keeping a drugstore? " He pulled a paper bag from his pocket, took out some red and black strands of licorice, solemnly handed her and Pete one each of red and black, nodded to them, and walked away.

" I guess you think Wilbur Baker's a little weird, Pete, but he isn't. He's just different, and you have to get to know him. He's Billy Baker's grandfather, and he's very good, and all the college students come and talk to him about themselves. Lots of times when some famous Friend comes to visit Halford and talk at the college, people from Philadelphia or from London Meeting, they know about Wilbur Baker and want to meet him. He usually carries licorice around and has a special joke for everybody, like that ' Has thee got a pain? ' business. His store is lovely. Have you seen it yet? It's old-fashioned, with those big, colored-glass jars in the window and little round tables. His wife is dead, and his son, Johnny Baker, Billy's father, was killed in an automobile accident a couple of years ago. Billy's mother,

Ginny — the one over there in the blue dress — helps run the store — "

" It's all right with me! " Thank goodness Pete had interrupted; Jane had begun to feel as if she couldn't stop talking. " I don't know why you have to apologize if Wilbur Baker's a character. I like characters. I even like plain speech; some of the old-timers in New York still use it to everyone, and we sometimes do, at home."

" We never did at home much, except Dad to me when I was little. But Eleanor Digges, even when she goes to Columbus or somewhere, says ' thee ' to traffic policemen, bus drivers, and everybody. They probably think she's wacky."

" You certainly are a sociable type, Cousin Jane, aren't you? " said Pete, and grinned.

" Oh, well — Eleanor — "

" Why wouldn't you go with your pop and eat up Eleanor's little, nice brown chicken, the way she wanted you to? "

She ought to have gone. There wasn't anything much to eat at home, and it would have been a good chance to talk to Eleanor about learning to keep house. Still, it would be easier to bring it up without Dad there, watching to see if she was being polite enough. Anyhow, it certainly wasn't any of Pete's business whether she felt like having Sunday dinner with Eleanor or not!

Just then, Billy and Nancy Mead, who had been hanging around at a little distance, walked up to them, Billy looking pudgier than ever in his crumpled summer suit. The braces on Nancy's teeth were as hideous as usual. Nancy was pretty fat too, and was always laughing and yelling about something in her screechy voice.

" These are the Meads, Pete — I mean, it's my cousin Pete — they're at Halford School too — " How did people ever learn to make introductions without feeling embarrassed and sounding like idiots?

Nancy began asking Pete a lot of silly questions, and Billy said, " Have you heard anything from Mary Lee, Jane? She said she might write me, but she didn't. I guess she doesn't have much time."

" No, she hasn't even sent me a post card since she went to Young Friends." Jane knew her voice didn't sound very friendly, but after all, Billy could have been polite enough to ask her something about how she liked living at the cottage. As for Mary Lee, everyone at Halford School knew Mary Lee Stebbins wasn't interested in pudgy Billy, who was only fifteen anyway — except enough to keep him interested in her, because that was the way she was with boys. No wonder Larry Carmichael, with whom she went steady, was always jealous. But even Larry didn't mind Billy.

" Dad's waiting in the car for us," said Nancy Mead rather wistfully. " Come on, Billy. So long, Jane — tell Pete about our barbecue. I want him to come when we have it."

" I'll come to anything! " said Pete. " Who are they, Jane? " he asked as the Meads got out of earshot.

" Oh, their father has a big dairy farm about fifteen miles out of Halford. We sometimes hike out there, cross country, and then it's only about seven miles. The Meads are Friends; that's why Billy and Nancy go to Halford School, but mostly they hang out with the farm kids that go to Maryville Central. I'm a little bit sore at Billy right now. He isn't very polite. And I'm kind of mad at Nancy too. I heard something mean she said about me to someone, and I've been mad at her ever since school closed, but she acts as if nothing was the matter."

Pete looked at her for a minute in a queer way, then called to his mother: " Say, Uncle Julian's having his Sunday dinner here in Halford. Can't Jane have hers with us at Greenlands?"

"Of course she can, darling. What a good idea! Let's go collect the children and leave; I think I've met everybody."

"Oh, no, Marion Greene, I — I'd rather not — I mean, I can't!"

"No? Won't you really, dear? Well, get in the car anyway, and we'll give you a ride home."

"No — honest, Marion Greene, I don't want a ride. I mean, I'd rather walk — I like to walk." Maybe Marion Greene thought she had hinted to Pete to be asked, or something awful like that. After so much trouble to get out of going to Eleanor's house, here she was being forced to go to Greenlands, which was worse. It didn't seem to occur to anyone that it was terrible for a sensitive person to have to do something like that. If she accepted the ride, she would have to go through the argument again. It was beginning to seem, now, as if all she wanted was to be alone, even if it was only in her little bedroom at the cottage with its sloping ceiling and flaking whitewash. Or better still, to be outdoors with Kai, where things never seemed so bad. Dogs never tried to make her do things she didn't want to do. "It's a pretty walk, Marion Greene, and not far. I like it."

"O.K.," said Pete suddenly. "You take the car, Mother, and I'll walk with Jane."

"Oh, Pete — don't do that, please!" Marion Greene sounded really upset — how queer! — and put her hand on Pete's arm. "Darling, let Jane walk if she prefers to, but you come back with me. Rachel will have dinner on."

"She won't. I heard you tell her to wait till two o'clock. Don't fuss, Mother; I won't be late. Come on, Jane, if you're coming." As they walked off, Marion Greene stood looking after them.

Chapter V

W AS Pete going to walk to the cottage with her? Jane tried to match her steps to his long stride. Or would he leave her where the cottage driveway branched off from Halford Road and continue along to Greenlands by the road? His face looked scowling and angry, but his pace slackened a little when they came to the end of Meeting-house Street, where open country began and the dande-lions grew thick and gold by the wayside. What was it that made Pete seem different, more grown-up in a way, than most of the college boys? Was it because most of the Hal-ford students came from farms or small towns and Pete lived in New York and went to Europe almost every summer?

"Pete, did you ever see Venice?" She hadn't meant to be the first one to say anything if he was going to be sulky because his mother had tried to boss him, or whatever the reason was. But thinking of Europe had reminded her sud-denly of a travelogue she had once seen in the college gym-nasium about Italy; many of the views had shown a city that looked like a dream of water and stone and the flutter of pigeon's wings.

"See it? Sure!" Pete said, and seemed to pull himself out of his bad mood. "We've been there three or four times. Mother went to school in Rome for a while when she was about my age, and we know a lot of Italians. Venice is just like the pictures of it, Jane — sensational! Like a dream — you can't believe a city could look like that. I'd like to live there, have my own gondola, float around day and night — it wouldn't be bad! "

" I know what it is about you, Pete. You don't seem like a Quaker."

" I'm not a Quaker."

" Of course you are. Your mother and father are Friends, so you're a birthright Friend. You can't help but be."

" My mother was born an Episcopalian."

" So was mine. She became a convinced Friend after she married Dad. She met him when she was nineteen. She went to art school and she had her own car, and one day it broke down in front of Wilbur Baker's drugstore — " It was perfectly awful the way she kept on gabbing to Pete about all kinds of things that wouldn't be interesting to him! " But your Mother's a convinced Friend now, isn't she? "

" Oh, sure. She's like all the other people in the Meeting. You know the kinds of things they go in for. She's on a lot of committees that are always trying to do something about something — jails and slums and mental hospitals and wars. Don't get me wrong, Jane. I think all that's fine if you want to do it. Somebody has to! But Quakers aren't the only people that get worked up about things like that; they don't have any monopoly."

" Well — yes, I guess so. Only everyone knows that Friends do a lot more than anybody else — at least, when you figure there aren't very many of them, compared to other religions. Why, Quakers freed their slaves hundreds of years before it even occurred to anybody that you shouldn't have slaves. They were the first ones that started making a fuss about how people got treated in jails and hospitals and asylums — "

" I know. But that was a long time ago, and that's one of

the things that chills me off about the whole deal. Quakers are always harking back to something that happened 'way back, and taking the credit for it too! But they mostly live pretty soft now. You don't see them getting into real trouble for their principles, the way the early Friends used to, except for a few conscientious objectors that go to jail once in a while. They go on doing lots of things the same way they have for three hundred years."

"But you just said Friends *don't* do things the way they used to."

"What do you expect, consistency?" Pete smiled; he didn't seem to be annoyed at all at being picked up like that. "I guess living in a little Quaker town like this," he went on, "you don't even realize that most people think Quakers are peculiar. That's what a lot of it boils down to with me. I'm tired of being different. When I called my housemaster at school ' Matthew Nicols,' he thought I was being fresh. If you start explaining that George Fox said three hundred years ago that titles are wrong because people are equal — well, that goes over like a lead balloon with people who don't know anything about the whole thing, and how that business about titles fits into the whole philosophy. When the guys at school find out I'm a Quaker, it makes them nervous."

"Why does it?"

"Oh, I don't know. They get a kind of feeling that they don't know what to expect; they act embarrassed until they get to know me. It's very boring, and I don't want any part of it any more. I only go to Meeting for Worship once in a while because Mother goes into a tail spin if I don't. But she ought to understand. After all, she isn't a birthright Friend. Why, her father — my grandfather — is a retired general."

"A general!"

" Sure! " Pete laughed. He stopped by a fence that bordered the road. " It's no disgrace to have a general in the family. Say, who's this? "

" That's one of the Larkins cows — Bertha. She's pretty nice, but she's awfully nosy about anyone that goes along the road."

" Hello, Bertha! " Pete patted the brown nose thrust inquisitively over the fence. " Imagine a place where you even know the cows' first names! "

" That's only because the Larkinses are Friends, and we always get our butter and eggs from them. Your mother will too. But about your grandfather, Pete — I didn't *say* it was a disgrace. People aren't responsible for their grandparents. Both my grandfathers died before I was born, but the one that wasn't a Quaker — Jean's husband — had a factory and made parts for airplanes that were used in the war."

" My grandfather would like me to go to West Point."

" Oh, Pete! "

" Well — I'm not going to. Not because I think it's wrong, necessarily, but because I want to be a scientist. I like physics and math."

" Pete! You don't mean you'd ever go into the Army, even for a little while? "

" I'm not sure."

" But Quakers don't, because it's wrong to kill people, Pete. It has to be. It's always wrong, no matter who it is! Real Quakers work in mental hospitals instead, or drive ambulances, or even go to prison, the way you were saying, if their consciences won't let them register. Or they volunteer for trying new medicines, and when the war is over they go in with milk and things so the children won't starve — "

" Some Friends go into the Services."

"People used to be read out of Meeting for being soldiers — and I think they still should be. What about our peace testimony? The Indians never killed Quaker settlers because they knew Friends didn't carry guns and wouldn't rob them or hurt them."

"Jane, let's drop it. I don't know how we got into this, but it's something people have to decide for themselves. Dad was in one of the 'conscientious objectors' camps, but he doesn't try to influence me, because he knows it's a tough decision. It's easier for a girl, of course."

"I know I'm right!"

"You don't, though, that's the point. The world is full of millions of people who know they're right. You aren't old enough or experienced enough to know what you really think yourself, let alone telling other people what's right for them. You don't have to look sore. I'm not criticizing you. I'm only stating facts, that's all, and there's nothing to be sore about. It isn't your fault that you live in a little Quaker place. I guess if you have to be mixed up in a Meeting at all, it's kind of fun if it's such a little one that you know everybody in it."

"I know everyone in Meeting for Worship or Meeting for Business except when the fall semester starts and the freshmen come. They aren't all Friends, and some of the ones that are don't come to Meeting."

"I understand that. I feel I've had it, myself. Dad's active in the Meeting too, just like Mother, and I probably got too much stuffed down my throat too soon, starting with First Day School. See, even now I don't call it Sunday School."

"That was because the early Friends thought the names of the days and the months were heathenish —"

"I know. I've heard it all too, but the whole thing leaves me cold. First Day School, Young Friends, Meeting for Business, Quarterly Meeting, Yearly Meeting, Silent Meeting for Worship — silent! It wasn't so bad in your Meeting this morning. Having to be quiet gives you a chance to think about things that are on your mind, but in a big Meeting there's usually some long-winded character on his feet most of the time, droning on and on, and it's all supposed to be inspired! "

"Pete!" It couldn't be right for Pete to be talking like that; it wasn't even right for her to be listening to him, but it was interesting. Nobody at Halford School talked like that. Not that everybody who went there swallowed everything, the way Pete seemed to take for granted. Not by a long shot! After all, people were perfectly capable of thinking for themselves, even if they did live in a small place! Mary Lee Stebbins sometimes said she intended to marry out of Meeting and have a church wedding with music. Johnny Seaman wanted to go to Harvard — not Halford or Haverford or Earlham. But none of them talked about the Society of Friends the way Pete did. They all thought they were lucky to be birthright Friends. That was what Wilbur Baker always told them. He said it was a serious responsibility too. And Pete thought it was all just boring. He was walking beside her with his eyes fixed on the ground and scowling a little. Suddenly she realized that he must have followed her automatically when she had turned in at the cottage drive.

"This is the place, Pete — " She stopped a few steps from the front door. "Let's go around to the back; there's a path to Greenlands from the kitchen door. I'll show it to you; it's a short cut."

"Is this where you're living?" asked Pete, and he looked very surprised.

"Yes, this is the cottage."

Why was Pete inspecting it? Jane wondered. There wasn't anything interesting to see. From the front, it looked about as dreary as from the back, except that there was a little peaked gable over the front door that was rather nice and made it look a little bit like a house where dwarfs might live. The climbing rose that somebody had once planted by the front door looked almost dead. She might weed around it this afternoon. A couple of buds of late iris had come out since yesterday, by the edge of the drive. Iris could live through almost anything — they took care of themselves like wild flowers — but these needed dividing by now. Somebody must have liked the cottage once, and had had some kind of garden around it. There were three or four new instructors coming to Halford in the fall, with wives. She imagined the wife saying to her husband: " Oh, we must take the cottage, even if it is tiny! I don't care what we pay — look at the lovely grounds! "

" Hey, let's go in, Jane! Didn't you say you had to let Kai out? "

" He's in the house so he wouldn't follow us to Meeting. But, Pete, there's nothing to see inside. It's still a mess, with moving — "

Kai came bounding along the hall and lunged against the door. When she had opened it, there didn't seem to be any way of stopping Pete from walking calmly in. The hall looked awful, with loose clothes and things lying on the cartons. The study, into which Pete was now sticking his head, looked terrible too. Dad kept his papers and reference books all over the furniture and sometimes on the floor. Now the kitchen, which was the worst of all. Kai must have got on the table to lick the breakfast plates, because one was lying on the floor, broken.

" I guess you think it all looks pretty sloppy, Pete, but after all, we just moved in. It's taken all my time to help Dad put his books in the study and try to find out where things are in the kitchen, and having to go to Meeting this morning — "

" I wasn't thinking about that, Jane. I don't know why a kid your age should be able to keep house anyway."

" I'm no more of a kid than you, Pete! "

" I know, but you seem an awful lot younger. Now, don't get mad at me again. No; what I want to know is, why don't you have some of the stuff from Greenlands here? Something to sit on in the other room besides that broken-down armchair? And some kitchen gear in here? "

" Dad said we mustn't take anything except our clothes and personal things. He said that was what you do if you rent somebody your house furnished, and I think he's absolutely right! "

" I think he's running it into the ground. We didn't have any idea you were moving into such a — a little place."

" It is little — and it's pretty crummy too — but that doesn't mean that Dad and I have to accept favors from people we hardly even know."

" Calm down. Nobody's offered you any favors yet. Only, look, Jane — I want you to change your mind and come on over to Greenlands with me now."

" The reason I wouldn't accept a ride was because — "

" Was because you didn't want to go there. I know, but Mother isn't ever going to feel free to come here, if you make such a fuss, unless you go there first."

" Pete — I — well, I don't mean this the way it sounds, but I don't think she should come here. I'm going to fix the house up, but it still won't be the kind of place where you'd want company."

" Mother could help you make it nicer."

" Eleanor Digges is going to help me."

" Will she want to? I mean, why should she, if you always act the way you did after Meeting when she asked you to dinner? "

" Eleanor would do anything for me or Dad because of

the way she felt about Mother. She thought Mother was the most wonderful person that ever existed. Anyway, she's not sensitive."

" I bet you everybody's sensitive."

" Eleanor wouldn't miss a chance at housekeeping, even in someone else's house. She's always baking bread and making slip covers, things like that. She cuts recipes out of magazines and tries them, like muffins with nuts in them. She's got a little house now, with a lot of big furniture that used to belong to her family stuffed into it. She keeps it polished with something that smells like lemons. Everything's all cluttered up with a lot of little footstools and pictures of people Eleanor knows. As a matter of fact, I kind of like it. It feels safe."

" That's a peculiar thing to say."

" I guess it is. I probably do say a lot of peculiar things."

" Why do you? "

" I don't know. I don't think much about the reasons I do things or say them."

" Maybe you should." Pete pushed open the kitchen door and leaned in the doorway, his eyes on the overgrown yard outside. " In order to be able to understand other people."

" Lots of time I *don't* understand other people." Jane thought again of Eleanor crying at the Memorial Meeting and now planning to " pop in " at Greenlands as if nothing had happened. " Pete, when there was the Memorial Meeting for my mother I said to — to God — only not out loud, naturally — that I wasn't ever going to Meeting again unless my father absolutely made me go, and that if I had to go, I wouldn't even think about Him. At least, never until I could see why Mother had to die. Because I don't see why, and I never will, I don't think. If it was God's will — then, I'm against it, that's all."

Pete turned and looked at her, but he didn't seem

shocked or even surprised. Yet what she had told him was something she had thought she would never tell a soul.

" There wasn't any point to it, you know, Jane."

" What do you mean? "

" I mean, there's no point in saying things to God, because there isn't any God. I've had my doubts for a long time, anyway. You can't help but have, when you think about all the kinds of things that happen to people — and animals. Ever since something happened to me a while back, I haven't believed in God at all."

Jane thought suddenly of a time, years ago, when her mother, in a Columbus department store, had taken her into an elevator that went down very fast. Pete's words now were giving her exactly that same sick, sinking feeling deep down in her stomach. But why? Why should anything he said make her feel sick — bother her? Why should she pay any attention? Was it because what he said was something she had been thinking herself, only not — not consciously, not wanting to admit it? Was what she had been thinking and hoping all these months simply ridiculous — that God would eventually get, well, tired of her not worshiping him? And then he would give her what the grown-up Quakers called an " opening," that mysterious, indescribable something that could happen in your spiritual life. Even if it was only once that you had an opening, you never forgot it completely, and you felt peaceful and happy all the time afterward. Like Wilbur Baker, for instance, who in a way had not seemed to mind when the accident happened to his son, though John Baker's wife, Ginny, who had not even been in the car that overturned, got so sick when she heard that she almost died too.

" How did we get onto this? " asked Pete impatiently. " I guess because we've been to Meeting." He looked at his watch. " I guess I'd better be moving along or Mother will have my ears."

" Follow this path, Pete. It's pretty weedy, but you can't miss it, and it's much shorter than by the road."

" O.K. Now, Jane — for the last time. We're living in your house for the simple reason that Uncle Julian wanted to rent it. So are you going to go on sulking, or are you coming over? "

" Not until it's our house again. I suppose it seems silly to you."

" How right you are."

" It happens to be the way I feel."

" You could change the way you feel."

" No, I couldn't. That shows you don't understand. You're being arbitrary."

" Suit yourself! See you around — sooner or later."

Jane watched his tall figure for a moment as he sauntered down the path, then turned back to the kitchen. It looked dark after the sunlight outside; a greenish light filtered through the ivy that half obscured the windows.

" I'll heat up a can of chili, Kai, and give you some. You like chili." She tried to persuade herself that her voice sounded cheerful in the silence. " It'll be a picnic. It'll be fun! "

Chapter VI

"HERE are your Cokes, kids." Ginny Baker put the tray down on the little, round marble-topped table. "That one's yours, Mary Lee, and I put some fresh lemon in yours, Jane. I'll get Kai some water, poor thing. He's panting terribly." She went back to the fountain, humming to herself.

"Isn't it hot!" Mary Lee pushed her short, glossy brown curls back from her forehead and moved her glass to make the ice tinkle. "It's dopey to wear jeans in this weather. Ginny looks a lot cooler in that cotton dress than we do. She doesn't look old enough to be Billy's mother, does she?"

"I guess not. I like her, only —" Jane stopped speaking while Ginny brought a saucer of water, put it on the floor, and went back behind the big, carved wooden soda fountain.

"Only what?"

"She doesn't act sad any more, about John Baker. And they used to hold hands in the street, like — like you and Larry."

"Oh, well, it's been a couple of years since the accident."

"That shouldn't make any difference, just time going by."

"I don't know if it shouldn't. But it does, usually, I

guess. Anyway, people don't always act as sad as they feel. Now, I expected to find you kind of glooming around about having to move to the cottage, Jane."

" Well, it isn't that I *like* living there, Mary Lee! But it's only for the summer, and I'm fixing it up so we can rent it in the fall. I've made more of a start on the yard than I have inside. Dad did some digging where the grass was too thick for me to do it, and Verena Larkins said she'd give me some annuals, because it's too late to start any from seed."

" I ought to be on my way to the Larkinses' for eggs for Mother right now." Mary Lee glanced at the drugstore clock whose brass pendulum swung back and forth on the wall above them. " I never knew anyone else your age, Jane, who knew about gardening the way you do, knowing the names of things and everything. I suppose it's because your mother liked it."

It wasn't that, Jane thought, or not altogether. Gardening was important because flowers were beautiful. But the special way she felt about them was something she would never even want to try to explain to anyone — certainly not to Mary Lee, though Mary Lee was probably the nearest thing she had to a close friend.

" Now you're back, Mary Lee, will you play tennis sometimes? "

" I don't know; I won't have much time. I promised Mother if I could go to the conference, I'd help with the kids every day when I got back."

" You always do that anyhow."

" Oh, yes. Five dear little brothers and sisters — what a deal! What I mean is, I promised I'd take over a little more, get supper and take care of Juney and what not. I'm going to make Arline a couple of nice dresses for school; the poor kid's in rags, practically. Mother needs some rest. You know how she is — and she got really bushed while I was gone. So I'll be tied up a lot of the time."

"You can play tennis mornings."

"Sometimes, maybe, if it isn't too hot. I know you want to practice, Jane, but I'm not good enough for you."

"That's because you don't care. Your backhand's terrific sometimes. If you practiced — "

"But I *don't* care. That's just the point. I especially don't care about running around on a court when it's hot. Why can't summer and winter days be mixed up? You know, one of each in succession."

"What? Why you couldn't do that — "

"I know!" Mary Lee laughed. "Or I guess you couldn't. But it was a — a rhetorical question, Jane; I didn't expect you to answer. You always think people want to know the answer if they ask you something."

"How can you tell if people don't mean what they say?"

"Oh, for goodness' sake, most people know whether someone's kidding or not! It isn't anything you can explain. Listen, Jane, I really have to go to the Larkinses' in a minute, but I'm dying to hear about your relatives from New York. Mother and Dad said they're here and came to First Day Meeting."

"Relatives! You mean you want to hear about Pete. I knew you'd be asking about him the minute you got back."

"Well, what if I am! Jane, everyone isn't a tomboy like you, after they're about twelve. There's nothing so awful about being interested in boys. What am I supposed to do with my spare time — if I have any? There isn't anyone around this summer except little kids."

"Billy Mead was asking about you after First Day Meeting."

"Oh, goodness, Billy Mead! Billy doesn't even have any

way of getting to Halford from the farm unless his mother
or father has to come in for something."

" Well, why does there have to be anybody? What about
Larry? He's the nicest boy at Halford School, and you've
been going steady with him all your life."

" But Larry's at the lake for all summer, so what am I
supposed to do? I'm not going to eat your cousin up alive
or anything. I'm curious, that's all. What's he like? Is he
good-looking? "

" Yes, kind of. He looks like Ed Marshall a little bit, only
taller and thinner, but he's better-looking than Ed. Like a
movie star. I haven't seen his little sisters, but Dad has, and
he says they're pretty. But Pete's funny."

" Funny? How? "

" He doesn't like Halford. It's too small to suit him, or
not sophisticated enough, or something. He didn't want
his father to be president."

" He didn't, honest? "

" No. He likes to live in New York. He goes to Andover
and they all go to Europe in the summer. Pete wouldn't
want to go to a Quaker school, he said."

" Oh." Mary Lee looked impressed.

" That's almost all I know about him. I haven't seen him
since First Day. Dad's been over to Greenlands two or
three times, and he says Pete's doing some studying. So
then Dad hounds me about my algebra. I promised him I'd
work on it this summer. I still don't know why he thinks I
ought to be an all " A " student, just because he's a professor."

" I don't think it's that. He gets mad because you don't
try. Anyone that's in classes with you knows that you could
do better."

" Like you and your tennis."

" That's different altogether. Now about Pete. You know

him, so let's go over to Greenlands sometime tomorrow."

" I don't want to."

" Why not? "

" I can't explain it. You wouldn't understand."

" Oh, that's what you always say. Look, Jane, I can't go barging over there and say hello."

" Sure you can, if you're so anxious to meet him! "

" You know I can't. It isn't — well, it isn't even as if Dad was one of the faculty. You know — that might be kind of an excuse. But I couldn't go to Greenlands and walk in and say, ' Hi, I'm Mary Lee Stebbins, and my father runs the post office.' Especially when it's such a little post office."

" Oh, that's all silly."

" Why won't you go over, Jane? You haven't had a fight with Pete, have you? "

" No, I haven't! "

" Oh, come on, Jane. You know it's awfully easy for people to get mad at you — or to make you mad, I don't know which exactly. I remember last year, right after school started, you wouldn't even speak to me for about a week — and I still don't know why."

" I do! It was something that hurt my feelings."

" Well, whatever it was, let's not dig it up now."

" Anyway, I haven't had a fight with Pete. But he got a little sore, First Day, because I said I wouldn't go to Greenlands while they're living there."

" That's pretty asinine — your not going, I mean."

" No, it isn't. But you don't understand. The only person who does, kind of, is Dad. I was surprised."

" I suppose he minds other people living there more than you do."

" More! "

" Sure! Why wouldn't he? He's lived there a lot longer than you have — all his life! But about Pete — "

61

" Well — " Jane reflected. Pete was sulking, apparently, and the summer was turning out very boring, the way she had suspected it would. Dad was at the college library a good deal, and even Eleanor couldn't be at the cottage much, because she was doing some typing for him. " I tell you what, Mary Lee. I can't do anything today because I have to give Billy his tennis lesson; I promised. And after that Eleanor and I are going to try to whitewash the kitchen at the cottage; all the stuff is at her house and we'll take it to the cottage in her car. We could come here tomorrow, if you want to, and I could call up Pete and ask if he wanted to come to Halford and meet a friend of mine."

" That's awfully roundabout," Mary Lee began, just as Billy, coming out from the Bakers' quarters behind the store, racket in hand, climbed up on the fountain and took a flying leap that landed him at their feet with a crash of overturned chairs.

" Hi, Mary Lee! " He got up and shook himself. " I thought you were still away at Young Friends. Hey, Jane, did I hurt my racket any? "

" Did you hurt yourself any, Billy, that's more like it! " Jane said, then, " I think he's all right, Ginny," as his mother came rushing over.

" Oh, he always is! " Ginny cuffed his ear lightly. " I don't know what his bones are made of — rubber, probably. If you do it again, Billy, I'll ask your grandfather to make you stay out of the store altogether. Jane, Billy says you're going to play tennis with him again today. It's sweet of you, but I'm afraid it's awfully boring. I remember Ed Marshall telling me once that you're really good."

" For a girl, Ed said," Billy added. " I asked him, and that's what he said, that you're very good, for a girl. I wish Ed would come back from the lake."

" So do I," said Jane. It was natural that Billy should miss

Ed, who lived in rooms above the drugstore, rented from the Bakers. Everyone liked Ed! Even though he was about thirty, the Halford College girls were always trying to get him to ask them for a date. Ed always said that most girls only pretended to be interested in athletics!

"When this is my drugstore," said Billy, "I'll give free sodas to everybody who isn't twelve yet."

"Your grandfather practically does that as it is," said Ginny, "and it's a very long way from being your drugstore."

"I'll put in air conditioning" — Billy looked up at the ceiling fan that whirred above their heads — "and a big television set. Come on, Jane, let's go on over to the courts."

Mary Lee, who had gotten up to go, suddenly sank back down into her chair. "Hey, Jane! Who's that?"

Pete and his mother came in and walked right up to them. They'd probably been to Maryville, Jane thought. Wasn't it typical of the way things always happened where Mary Lee and boys were concerned! One good thing was that there wasn't any need to do more than start trying to introduce everybody, because Marion Greene was taking over, telling Mary Lee she had met her parents after Meeting, pulling two of the little tables together, ordering Cokes for everybody and saying hello to Billy and Ginny as if she'd known them for years!

Pete, who was sitting very casually, with his chair tilted back, was taking a good long look at Mary Lee. It was absolutely true what the other girls at school always claimed — that Mary Lee changed, somehow, the minute there was a boy around. She was pretty anyway, with her wide-set brown eyes and her tall, lovely figure. But when a boy showed up, you could almost feel a sparkle in the air between Mary Lee and him! How did she do it? Mary Lee always said that she didn't do anything — that she *certainly* never tried to attract a boy who was interested in anyone else — but the other girls never believed her. Neither did Larry. Sometimes he and Mary Lee would bust up — but never for long.

"You know, Pete, I was asking Jane about you the minute you walked in the door," Mary Lee was saying. "Well, of course, Halford's so small that any time there's a new faculty family we all just about go out of our minds with curiosity until we know what they're like."

"Oh," said Pete, and grinned. "This is confidential, of course, but we're sensational, all of us!"

Mary Lee laughed. "Jane says you go to Andover. What's it like? Do you like it?"

"Jane!" Billy stopped juggling tennis balls and pulled at her arm. "Aren't we going to the courts for my lesson?"

"Billy," said Marion Greene, "I want to talk to Jane for a minute or so first. Do you two play a lot?"

Billy nodded. "Ed Marshall — he's the athletics director — says Jane's better than all the college girls except maybe one or two."

Jane looked across the table to see if Pete had heard, but he was telling Mary Lee about taking his record player to school with him.

"Jane, dear," Marion Greene began, and Billy sighed and flopped down on the floor beside Kai, " — I want to talk over this matter of your coming to Greenlands. Your father has told me how you feel and so has Pete, and I understand. It must be one of the loveliest houses of its period in the country. Naturally it means a lot to you."

"You do kind of get used to a place if you've lived there all your life, Marion Greene."

"Of course you do. But I want you to make an effort just the same and come."

64

" I couldn't."

" I think you could if you tried, and I need your advice about the garden. Lonnie says you know as much about it as he does."

" Lonnie! "

" Yes, Rachel told me all about him, and that he was your regular gardener for years. We got hold of him, and he started work yesterday."

" Oh, that's wonderful! Dad felt terrible when he had to tell Lonnie that we — that we weren't going to have him any more, and I cried. We didn't know that you'd get him — or anybody — to take care of the garden. And Dad said you'd feel embarrassed if we tried to do it — I mean, if you looked out of the house and saw us doing the weeding or anything — because a tenant is entitled to privacy. Lonnie's so old that he doesn't work very fast, and he's deaf, but if you yell a little, he can always make out what you're saying. He's marvelous with the roses — he put in that square rose bed before I was born — "

" I don't know a thing about gardens, Jane, because I've always lived in cities, but I realize they mustn't be neglected. The Greenlands garden is my responsibility for the time being. I wouldn't let it come to harm any more than I'd let your furniture get damaged. But as to all these notions of your father's about privacy and tenants and so on — " She stopped abruptly.

She had probably stopped, Jane decided, because she'd been about to say something that would be a criticism of Dad. How glad he would be to hear that Lonnie was back, moving slowly among the beds and borders, drinking endless cups of coffee with Rachel in the grape arbor, and nevertheless getting everything done, the endless, patient digging, pruning, thinning, weeding, spraying that made the garden more beautiful every year! " I guess the day

lilies are blossoming now, Marion Greene, aren't they?"
The day lilies that every summer shone like gold flames
against the yew hedge!

"I'm afraid I don't know which they are, Jane. You'll
have to come and show me. We must be getting on.
Rachel's got my little girls on her hands. Isn't Rachel a
darling? She's been such a help in getting settled. I tell
you what, Jane. Pete and I and the twins are all going to
Columbus this weekend to stay with an old college friend
of mine who's married and settled there, but come and
have tea with us Monday."

"I don't know —" It was hard to say no outright to
Marion Greene! Her voice was warm and low and almost
— almost hypnotizing! Her eyes looked friendly; they were
the same clear gray color as Pete's, who otherwise didn't
look like his mother at all.

"Say yes, Jane! Or, rather, don't say it, but leave it open
and see how you feel about it when the time comes."

"Hey, Mom — Mary Lee's supposed to be getting eggs
at the Larkinses' for her mother. We'll go there now —
how about it? — and we can leave you at Greenlands and
I'll drive her back to Halford."

"Of course, sweetie, why not? We'll drop Jane and Billy
at the courts first."

"I'd rather walk, Marion Greene." A ride was no fun as
part of a whole mob!

There was a lot of milling around and talking as they all
left, and Pete tweaked her ear as he passed her. "See you
at tea next week, Jane!" So he had heard some of what she
and his mother were talking about!

Jane walked out of the drugstore and, together with
Billy, watched the Greenes and Mary Lee get into the
convertible.

"Some car!" said Billy. "Why wouldn't you let them

take us to the courts, Jane? There's plenty of room in back."

" I guess because I never do anything like anybody else."

" Oh, well, now can we go play tennis? "

" I'm all ready, Billy."

The car started up and glided away. Pete was driving. Mary Lee was sitting between him and his mother.

Chapter VII

K AI — this is the fourth day in a row it's rained all day."

Kai wriggled out from the spot behind the stove where he liked to sleep, though it was much too small for him, and padded heavily over to put his head in her lap.

A dog was better than nobody, but the cottage did seem lonesome when it rained! How dark the rooms were on a day like this, even though she had trimmed the ivy from the windows! Dad was at the library and Mary Lee's little brothers and sisters all had pinkeye or something. Even Eleanor was away, visiting her cousins in Hammond! Was Marion Greene really expecting her to tea this afternoon? She might have forgotten all about giving the invitation in the drugstore the other day. Not that it mattered, since she wasn't going anyhow. But what was there to do? It was too wet for tennis, too wet and cold for swimming or working on the cottage grounds, and it was only three o'clock. Supper was all ready; she had made the tuna-fish casserole as Eleanor had shown her, and it only needed to be put into the oven. Eleanor had said not to try to put the enamel on the bathroom walls while it was so wet outside. Perhaps she should light the copper boiler and have a hot bath and read in the tub. But gas was expensive, and the tub was a very peculiar shape, and small, not like the huge Greenlands bathtubs, with mahogany around them.

She ran to the front door because a car had come up the drive with a roar and stopped short. It couldn't be Jean, but it must be, because nobody else drove like that!

Right away everything seemed much less miserable and lonely. Jean slid out from behind the wheel, put up an umbrella patterned in spring flowers to match her raincoat, and rushed into the cottage.

" Oh, Jean! I thought you were still in Europe! " Jean's kiss was always lovely-feeling because of the perfume she used and the cool softness of her cheek, even though it was never a real kiss, because of lipstick; she just pressed her face against yours for a moment. " It's marvelous to see you, Jean! Come on into the kitchen; there's no place else to sit down."

" Oh, my lamb! " Jean stopped short in the kitchen and looked around her. " I only remembered the cottage vaguely. I didn't realize it was like this! Oh, my poor baby! "

" It's just for the summer — "

" But all the same, your father's letter didn't give me any real idea — " Jean sat down in the rocker. " Where is he? "

" At the library. You didn't telephone you were coming. We didn't even know you were in Columbus."

" I left France day before yesterday. Something about Julian's letter worried me, and I thought I'd better fly back and see what was going on. But this is worse than I expected, Janey. My poor little cricket! "

It was nice of Jean to mind so much, Jane thought; even if it was a little embarrassing to have her carry on quite so much in her soft, fluting voice. The cottage kitchen already looked a little nicer with the checked cotton curtains

Eleanor had helped her hem, but it would seem like a hovel to Jean, whose big Columbus apartment was so fancy, with maids who wore uniforms, and fresh flowers always being sent in by a florist, and Jean's friends coming and going in the big living room that she was always having done over.

"Shall I make you some coffee, Jean? I know how. Or tea?"

"Nothing, darling, not a thing. I can't bear either without cream. My diet, you know!"

That sounded familiar. Jean always was on a diet because she was terrified of getting fat. Dad used to get annoyed because she talked about it so much on her visits to Greenlands when Mother was alive. But it was reasonable for Jean to fuss about things like that, because she really was still quite pretty and slender.

"Are you doing the housework in this desolate little place? Where's Rachel?"

"She's at Greenlands, working for the New York Greenes."

"Oh, yes — Julian said they'd taken the house. They must be the ones your mother visited that year she joined me in Paris. She liked them, I remember. Marion especially. But I simply can't bear to think that you should be forced out of the house that ought to be your natural background. Why, when your mother told me she was engaged — " She stopped. Jean was talking just like Dad, Jane thought; she was taking it for granted that a person who happened to be young didn't catch on to the simplest things. Greenlands had helped her grandmother get over her disappointment at having her beautiful, talented only daughter marry a professor at a small college.

"If only your father could have gotten the presidency at least!" Jean said.

"He's not an administrator, Jean. That's what he says

himself. He likes to teach and do research. He's working on some articles now too. The kind of thing he used to be able to sell to magazines and newspapers before Mother got sick and everything."

"Does Julian think he's going to be able to run Greenlands on his teaching salary and the income from articles? He must be fathoms deep in debt."

"Well — we've got plans about Greenlands." Jane felt her heart sink. They did owe money, she knew, though Dad had never said very much about it. He had never wanted to accept any from Jean, he had once explained, because most of it came from the factory Grandfather had owned and was made from war profits. Everyone always said Dad was a man of principle. But the factory did belong to someone else now, and it was all quite awhile ago! Jean gave money away to charities, but Dad said that was different from accepting it to use for things like doctors' bills or mortgages.

"Honey, I have a plan myself," said Jean, looking a little nervous. "It's something I've brought up with your father two or three times and he's always said no. But I think I should bring it up with you, and I think Julian would have to give in if you said it was what you wanted. I'd like you to live with me altogether, Jane. A girl needs to grow up with a woman in the household — and I'd love to have you, sweetie. You wouldn't be cut off from your father at all; you'd visit him or he could visit us. You'd live with me and go to school abroad or in Columbus, wherever we happened to be."

"I — I didn't have any idea you'd ever asked Dad if I could do that!"

"Well, I have, more than once. I've told him, too, that if we make this arrangement, you'll come into whatever money I leave, and I'll buy Greenlands now and put it into condition. He would have the right to live in it all his life, but you'd have it after him, darling. It's your house; you're entitled to it."

"Goodness, Jean, I'm so staggered —" It was a fantastic idea, but it would certainly solve a lot of things! How sensational it would be to be able to tell everyone at Halford School that she was going to live with her grandmother, and that she would be a kind of heiress and the owner of Greenlands! Jean wouldn't even want her to go to Meeting, and didn't care about her grades. "It's so middle-class, Julian!" Jean had said once, when Dad was fussing about her Latin or something. If she was away most of the time, Dad would probably be glad to see her when she came for a visit.

"We could leave right away, Jane. I've got nothing to keep me here. I've been promising my beloved Mirailles a visit for ages; they'd adore to have me bring you. They have the big house near Aix, and the girls are about your age. You'd have a heavenly time."

"I remember about them. But didn't you say last year those girls are about eleven or twelve?"

"Around that, I think."

"But —" Jane began, and stopped. There wasn't any point in reminding Jean that she was nearly sixteen.

"Now, another thing I want you to consider, darling. I suppose your father feels that in any case you'll come into the money sooner or later, since I don't have anyone else close to me to inherit it."

"Oh, Jean, Daddy never has said anything like that. Besides —" She broke off. Dad would certainly never want her to accept the money if he wouldn't take any of it for himself or for Mother, but perhaps Jean wouldn't understand that or believe it. She felt hot and uncomfortable.

"You won't have it, Jane, unless you do fall in with this

plan. It sounds awful to say this, but if you grow up under Julian's influence, you'd only give it all away. You know I believe in charity, Jane, and I give regularly to all sorts of causes, but you have to keep a sense of proportion about these things. If you don't, you end up with something like this place!" She looked around at the kitchen. "This dreadful little hut, and you, my poor little cricket, trying to scrub and cook — "

"Eleanor's helping me. I've got a casserole in the refrigerator she showed me how to make."

"Eleanor Digges! Yes, I suppose she's clucking over you like a hen! Well, Jane? What about it, darling? You'd have to come to Columbus with me right away so we could see about your passport and a reservation."

"Jean, I'd love to, but I can't. I absolutely can't." Jane was surprised to hear herself say it so positively. It wasn't what she thought she had been thinking at all. When it came right down to having to tell Jean yes or no, it wasn't possible to say anything but no. "It's Dad. That's the only reason. I couldn't go; he has to have someone." His old jacket was hanging on the kitchen doorknob, looking very shabby and limp, and there were worn leather patches on the elbows.

Jean nodded; she seemed to understand. "All right, Jane. You're a good youngster. I wish you could see your way to it, but it's all right. It's hard for him, it's hard for all of us, isn't it? Without Jessica." She got up. "I'll be going; I won't wait to see Julian. I'll be abroad till early fall, most likely."

"Then I'll come for a visit, Jean. For a week, maybe, or longer. Dad will let me. I know he will. I'll explain that I'm old enough to decide some things for myself now."

When Jean was gone, the cottage seemed gloomier than ever. The rain was still coming down. Jane looked at the kitchen fireplace. The thing to do would be to collect some wood, keep it dry in the cellar, and have a fire on days like this. Poor Jean had been too cold to take her coat off.

Jane wondered if she felt sorry about having refused Jean's offer, or if she would feel sorry later. It didn't, somehow, seem to be a matter of sorry or not sorry, exactly, but something that decided itself the way it did.

The front door creaked open and her father came in, shaking the drops from his big black umbrella. " What a day! " He stopped and sniffed. " Has Jean been here? That's her perfume, isn't it? "

" Yes, she just left."

" I thought so. She's back from France, then? "

" Yes. She came mostly, I guess, because of the letter that you wrote about us living here."

" Why didn't she wait to see me? She had the car, I suppose; she could have come in to Halford and looked me up at the library, for that matter."

" She came because of the letter, but it was me she wanted to talk to, Dad."

" Oh? " He sat down, looking at her suspiciously. " What about? "

" About — about kind of adopting me, and having me live with her and be an heiress. And — and about buying Greenlands and fixing it all up — for — "

" For me — as long as I live."

" Yes, and then — "

" Then it would come to you. I know, because she's brought this up a couple of times since your mother died. But I didn't know she would talk to you about it directly. What did you say, Jane? " Dad's voice sounded calm, but he didn't look calm.

" Oh, well, if I'd gone, I guess I certainly couldn't have

taken Kai — you know how Jean doesn't like dogs."

"No, Kai wouldn't do in the apartment, especially when the living room's in one of its all-white phases. Remember the time at Greenlands when Kai brought Jean the dead skunk?"

It was perfectly easy to tell that Dad wasn't thinking about Kai and the skunk. He was feeling awfully glad that she hadn't decided to live with Jean, only he didn't know how to say it!

"Perhaps I should have told you about these offers of Jean's, but in one sense I didn't take them seriously. She means it, of course; she wants you, but your natural place is here in Halford with me. And then, Jean's way of life, her standards of value, are different from mine, Jane —"

"Does that mean that, well, that Jean's wrong — automatically?" Jane took a deep breath. "I mean, Pete was saying something like that, after Meeting for Worship, when we walked back here — that it's hard to know."

"If your convictions are right?" Dad was looking embarrassed. This was the nearest thing to a personal conversation they had ever had.

There was a sudden banging on the closed kitchen door, and a confused, high-pitched shouting outside it. Jane opened the door and looked down at two tiny, drenched figures in wet play suits, who pushed their way into the kitchen, shouting.

"We got out!"

"When Mommy wasn't looking!"

"Or Rachel!"

"We went for a walk, but we're lost!"

"We want Mommy!"

"Jane, it's the Greene twins, Candy and Sandy." Dad raised his voice to carry over the children's shouts. "I'll call Marion."

Jane snatched the kitchen towel to dry the children's faces, wet with rain; their satiny cheeks glowed under the scrubbing. They had gray eyes with long lashes like Pete's, and silky dark hair, which sprang into curls as Jane rubbed it dry.

"Marion will be frantic, if she's missed them, to think of them out in this downpour." Dad picked up the telephone. "I'll tell her to drive over and get them."

"No!" Jane felt a sudden, surprising wave of resolution in her heart. The twins, with shrieks of delight, had hurled themselves on Kai; children and dog were wriggling in a happy heap on the floor. "I'll walk them home, Dad, under your big umbrella, so they can get into dry clothes. You call Marion Greene and say that I'm bringing the children."

Chapter VIII

WE ALWAYS go in the kitchen way."

"And Rachel says: 'Oh! My clean kitchen floor!'"

"You go on around to the back if you want to, Candy and Sandy." Resolutely Jane pressed the front doorbell.

"We'll stay with you and Kai."

The door opened. "Janey, honey!" Rachel's arms enfolded her. "I've been listening for the bell since Mr. Greene called up. Candy and Sandy, you hustle right on up to your room this minute, and I'll come up and change you into dry clothes. The idea, running out into the rain like that when my back was turned! Go on — I'll be right there." She shooed the twins off. "Kai, don't you go putting your big, muddy paws on my skirt! Janey, you go into the living room and dry off by the fire, and I'll tell

Mrs. Greene you're here. Would you believe it, I've been meaning to get over to the cottage every single day to see how you and your daddy were making out, but there hasn't been one minute to spare." She drew Jane into the living room. " Don't you have anything better to wear, weather like this than that raggedy old raincoat? "

" It's the only one I have, Rachel."

But Rachel was already bustling out of the room. " I'll tell Mrs. Greene you're here; she's upstairs somewhere, supervising that fellow from Maryville with the machine."

What on earth did that mean? Jane stared after Rachel, feeling a little dazed. How calm and ordinary Rachel was acting! Absolutely beaming all over, and perfectly cheerful and satisfied, and talking to the twins the same way she used to talk to Jane!

Anyhow, it was a bit of good luck to have a couple of minutes to get used to being at Greenlands, and in the most beautiful room of all. Still standing, Jane looked around her. Yes, it was different. But why? Nothing had been changed around, as she had half expected. The wood fire on the hearth burned high and bright; its flames shone on the brass andirons and threw gold lights on the white marble of the mantel. The French doors that led to the terrace and the garden were covered with curtains that matched the silk green-and-white drapes at the windows. Someone must have found the matching curtains in the attic. On the long table behind the old green velvet sofa stood the crystal punch bowl filled with yellow roses, their scent almost flowing from them and mingling with the pungent smells of wood smoke and furniture polish. Aside from some magazines and books in bright jackets on the table, there was nothing else that looked as if it belonged to Pete or his mother. Where was Pete, incidentally?

" Hi, Jane! " Marion Green came in, carrying the big,

round silver tray. "Why aren't you sitting down by the fire? Look, I'll put the tea things here. You can reach them from that hassock while you're getting warm and dry. Rachel's made scones; I told her this morning I hoped you were coming. Kai's upstairs with the twins. Thank you for bringing them back — little nuisances!"

"Oh, that's all right." Jane sat down, feeling trapped and shy. "I — I didn't mind. I might have taken a walk anyway."

"They've gone wild here; I suppose all the space around the house goes to their heads. Candy has a tiny black mole on her cheek — perhaps you noticed — so you *can* tell them apart." Marion Greene lifted a silver cover and began to butter the scones.

"Oh, I only came to bring the little girls back, Marion Greene. I mean" — Jane felt her cheeks getting hot — "I wasn't intending to stay. I'm not terribly hungry and I'm pretty busy — my grandmother was just here to see me. I know you said something about coming over to-day —"

"Your grandmother? But she's gone again?" Marion Greene sounded very calm, as if she hadn't noticed how idiotic and flustered-sounding Jane was. But it *was* hard to talk to strangers!

"Yes, she's gone. Jean never stays in Halford very long."

"Then you have time for a scone, haven't you, and a cup of tea? Or milk, if you'd rather, and here's hot toast and jam. Rachel will be hurt if you don't eat anything."

"Well, I like tea O.K." Jane, accepting the cup, saw that it was from the blue-and-white Wedgwood set. There were only two cups and saucers on the tray, so Pete wasn't expected.

"Your mother joined your grandmother for a while when she was abroad that time, didn't she?"

"Yes. Jean — everyone calls her Jean — had an apartment in Paris then."

"It would have been a chance for you, of course, but no, I think Julian was right."

"Daddy? Right about what?"

"Why, Jessica wanted to take you with her."

"She did? I never knew that."

"Oh, yes. I remember her telling me so in New York."

How peculiar, Jane thought, to find out something like that, something really important, at this late date! Because it *was* important. Mother *had* wanted to take her along. There had been times when Jane was unable to understand how Mother could have gone from her for almost a year!

"Was it — was it Daddy who stopped it? He never likes to have me see Jean a lot."

"So I've gathered. Your father thought too that your schoolwork shouldn't be interrupted and that neither Jessica nor Jean would have time to help you with school in another country and another language. And he would have been lonesome without you."

"Did he say that? Is that true?"

Marion Greene laughed. "Why shouldn't it be?"

"I didn't know. I mean, I'm glad I do know. Did Lonnie say things are O.K. in the garden?" Maybe that was changing the topic too fast and sounded peculiar, but she didn't want to start discussing anything personal with Marion Greene. Though it seemed that Dad had!

"Yes, he's not here today because of the rain, but he said to tell you to come and see the perennials. He said the winter was so snowy they'd come through all right. Have I got it straight?"

"Snow is good. It's when the ground is bare and heaves up and down with frosts that the roots get hurt. What's

78

that?" A faint, strange roar from upstairs had sounded suddenly louder.

"Oh, I've got someone in to sand down the floors and refinish them; he must be in the upstairs hall now. You know, my dear, that's one reason I've wanted you to come, so that I could show you I'm being careful with your lovely house. Rachel and I are doing the routine things, like cleaning windows and washing curtains and scrubbing woodwork. Naturally, a house as big as this got out of hand a little during Jessica's illness, and then you were alone to cope with it, with Rachel only part time. I imagine Julian's not very practical about housekeeping. If there's any way I can help you out at the cottage —"

"Oh, I guess we can make out all right at the cottage." That sounded rude, but it did seem as if Marion Greene was hinting that she would like to come over. Dad had been saying they should invite her and Pete. But look at the way Jean had reacted to the cottage!

"I'd love to show you our house in New York someday."

"Your house? I thought you lived in an apartment!"

"Goodness, no! We have a house your Uncle Charles and I bought not long after we were married, and did over. It's small, not one of the big town houses, but we all adore it. It's rented now, to one of the Columbia faculty families."

"Well, maybe you could come over to the cottage someday after Eleanor Digges and I get it fixed up. She's helping me with it so we can rent it in the fall when we —"

"When you're back here," said Marion Greene matter-of-factly. "I wonder —" she began, then stopped short as if she had changed her mind about whatever she was going to say. "Eleanor Digges has been here two or three times to call. I'm glad, because she's told me a lot I need to know about the college and Halford Meeting. She'll be the twins' teacher this fall, so meeting her gives them self-confidence about a new school — " She jumped up with an exclamation and ran out into the hall; shrieks and a rattling sound were followed by a crash. Jane hurried after her, and at the foot of the stairs helped pick up the two little girls who were sprawled in a heap, Kai circling worriedly around them.

" Oh, they've been sliding down the stairs on that old black tin tray with the daisies; I used to do that too! You slow down at the curve, but then you get going too fast — I hope they aren't hurt."

" We aren't hurt."

" We're hurt enough for being kissed! "

" It used to make me black and blue." But the twins had lovely, plump little arms and legs, Jane thought, as she followed them and their mother back into the living room. Eleanor Digges had said once, " Thee was never chubby exactly, Janey, even as a baby." She had probably been all angles from the minute she was born, just the way she was now.

The twins sprawled on the hearthrug and chattered.

" Could we have Kai? " Candy asked. " Maybe he'd like to live here. This house is lots bigger than your house."

" Jane doesn't like you to say that," reproved her twin. " She's mad, I guess. You can see her freckles more."

" All right, girls, that's enough." Marion Greene's voice was firm, but calm. She didn't seem to think it was terrible of the twins to talk like that.

" Let's have no more about dogs. People don't give their dogs away. Or about houses, either; this *is* Jane's house."

" How can it be? She lives in a little house."

" With Uncle Julian. We found it when we got lost."

" We're borrowing Jane and Uncle Julian's house for a while. And don't make personal remarks, either. That means, don't say things about how people look unless you're saying something nice. Or nobody will love you. How would you like that?"

"Don't you love us?"

"I guess you probably love us anyhow!"

The two little girls plunged into their mother's lap and began to kiss her with squeals and giggles. Jane watched the scene, and wondered why it made her feel sad. Had she ever behaved the way the twins were doing now? Not with Dad, certainly. He didn't even kiss her good night now, the way he used to when she was little. With Mother sometimes, when she was about the twins' age.

"Babies, run up to your playroom now, so I can visit with Jane in peace. You may have two cookies each. Leave Kai here." Marion Greene smiled, watching the children trot out of the room. "I call the big front bedroom their playroom, Jane, but I had that painted Italian furniture moved out of it and some sturdier things put in so they can romp around. Something I would like to do would be to have the white paneling in this room repainted, but I don't like to suggest it to your father. I have a feeling he might be offended. Do you think so?"

"Yes!" Jane felt a spasm of anger. Why should Marion Greene jump to the conclusion that Jane wasn't every bit as proud as her father! "We aren't the kind of people that want a lot of favors done for them. We don't want to have to feel obligated, and it isn't fair, just because you happen to be rich! I wish you wouldn't do any of those things — the garden, when you don't really care about it, and the floors and the woodwork! If — if the house isn't good enough for you — Oh! I knew I shouldn't come here!" She got up and started for the door. "I knew it all along and I said it all along. So now I've made a mess of it — like everything I ever try to do!"

It was still raining outside as she ran out the front door, her eyes prickling. Somebody grabbed her arm and held it firmly when she tried to pull it away. " Jane! " It was Pete, in a yellow slicker, but bareheaded.

" Let me go, Pete! " He must have just driven up; the car stood at the foot of the steps. If only she could have gotten away a minute sooner —

" What's all this about? "

" Nothing. I'm going home! "

" In this rain? Don't be silly. It's all right, Mother," he called to Marion Greene, who now appeared in the doorway and looked anxiously at them. " I'll drive her to the cottage."

He pushed Jane into the car; Kai tumbled hastily in after them, and they started down the drive. He smiled at Jane as she turned to glare at him. "Are you going to open the door on your side and jump out? I can't stop you."

" If — if a person happens to feel like walking home in the rain, that isn't any reason for shoving a person around."

" Push Kai's nose off the accelerator, will you, and tell me why you came bolting out of Greenlands like a rabbit."

" I — I got upset and lost my temper, the way I do sometimes when I don't mean to, and I was rude to your mother. She probably thinks I'm feeble-minded."

" Usually Mother can get along with anybody — it's almost a speciality of hers."

" She *was* trying to be tactful."

" Well, what was the problem, then? "

" It's very embarrassing to have people do a lot of things for you, like your mother fixing up Greenlands, when you can't do anything for them, and yet you can't stop them doing things."

" Oh, is that it? " Pete whistled thoughtfully to himself as he turned the car in at the cottage drive. The leaves of the thick-grown trees brushed the car roof. At the cottage he switched off the ignition and turned around to look at Jane. " I don't suppose you'd feel pleased, either, if we let the house go to pot. And as a matter of fact, there's something you could do, but Mother's scared to ask you in case you might feel insulted or something equally ridiculous."

" What is it? "

" She needs someone to take care of the twins, a couple of hours a day, or sometimes longer."

" Oh, Pete! I'll do that — I'd like to! I like little kids. I help with the Stebbins kids sometimes for the fun of it."

" A dollar an hour, for the twins."

" Oh, no. I wouldn't take any money for doing it."

" You have to, or Mother can't ask you to do it. It's a regular job, and it would be a terrific favor to her to have somebody responsible take over once in a while. Don't you see, Jane? If she pays you, then some days she could ask you to take them a little longer."

" She could still do that. I don't need the money."

" Save it for fall clothes, then, when school starts. Don't girls always get a lot of clothes every September? "

" I don't care about clothes! " Though having some money coming in would solve the problem of buying paint and curtain materials for the cottage. And Eleanor said nothing would make the bathroom floor look all right except some good linoleum. " Well, I'd like to get my racket restrung, Pete, and I don't like to ask my father for the money for that." This was true. If she said it was for things for the cottage, Pete might be sorry for her.

" O.K., fine. Come on over tomorrow when you finish breakfast and get the kids. I'll tell Mom."

" I'd feel silly coming over after rushing away like this."

" Take your choice. I bet you'll feel sillier if you don't. Come on, make up your mind."

83

"Pete, maybe I shouldn't ask you, but how come you don't look after the twins yourself?"

"I do sometimes." The rain and the trees darkened the car interior, but Jane could see that his face looked suddenly gloomy. "I have to spend a lot of time on schoolwork."

"Oh." *Had* Pete flunked some courses, then? The way he had talked about majoring in science the day they met hadn't sounded like it. But he looked as if he didn't want to discuss it any more.

"Yes or no, Jane? Look, if you don't want the job, I'll try Mary Lee again. She couldn't quite figure out how she was going to work the time —"

"Did you ask Mary Lee to help with the twins?"

"I brought it up, but nothing definite. Mother wanted to ask you first."

"All right. Tell her I'll be over about ten. I'll have to do the dishes and make the beds here first."

"Fine."

"I've got to go in and get supper now." Jane reached for the car door handle, then paused. "Were you just over at Mary Lee's, Pete?"

He nodded. "I've gone over to watch TV a couple of times. You have to brush those little kids away from in front of the screen."

"Mary Lee said the kids have pinkeye."

"They do, that's right. But a guy has to find some risks for excitement in Halford."

"See you tomorrow, Pete." Jane got out of the car and twisted her fingers into Kai's collar as they went into the cottage. I'll buy you a collar, Kai, because this one's almost worn out. A new red one, maybe, with the money from my job."

Yes, that was why she could stand the idea of going to

Greenlands every day. To earn money, Jane told herself. For the cottage, and for having her racket restrung, and for Kai's collar. Things like that.

Chapter IX

CANDY and Sandy! Sit down and stay put a minute! Don't go too near the water! " Jane dropped down on the grassy bank and looked at Stepping Stones pond; the surface of the water was smooth and silky in the glint of the morning sun. It was warm. The chilly rain had stopped during the night. The twins could have brought their bathing suits. It would be fun to teach them to swim, and their mother had said it was a wonderful idea. But it would have been awful to have them catch colds on her first day of taking care of them. They seemed perfectly happy now, excitedly setting up housekeeping under a shelving rock with the rag dolls they had lugged along from Greenlands.

" Here's a mushroom, Marybelle, a *real* mushroom; you can have it for lunch for a treat," said Candy impressively, and put the mushroom in her doll's lap. " They grow in the woods."

Sandy was picking ferns to decorate the "house." It must be because they were city children, Jane thought, that every little thing was so thrilling to them. The narrow woods path to the pond, slippery with pine needles, had excited them so much they had rushed around like a couple of puppies.

Kai suddenly sat up, pricked up his ears, and growled.

" Jane! " Candy tugged at her arm. " There's somebody coming out of the woods! " She pointed across the pond.

" It's Pete! " yelled Sandy.

"Hi, kids! Hi, Jane!" He was wearing jeans and a thick, white ribbed sweater, and carrying a towel and a book, Jane noticed. Was he going to cross over to them? But when he stepped on the first flat rock of the series that crossed the pond, the twins jumped up and ran over the slippery rocks to him.

"Candy! Sandy!" Jane ran after them. "Don't ever, ever do that again. You could fall in the pond! Pete" — he was sitting down now, and trying to disengage himself from the twins, who were clinging around his neck — "the current from the brook is strong through the middle of the pond, and it's deep in places —"

"Not deep enough," Pete said. "I tried diving off that big rock and almost knocked myself out on the bottom."

"That's really dangerous. You can't tell where it's deep and where it isn't by looking, and there are rocks on the bottom in some places. You have to know the pond to dive here. Arline Stebbins almost got drowned once when she and Billy Baker came here and didn't have anyone older with them."

"Look, you two little chumps," Pete addressed the twins. "You do what Jane tells you, do you hear? And don't cross the stones again unless she says you can."

The twins nodded absent-mindedly; they were watching Kai, who was pacing up and down on the opposite bank, anxious to join them but disliking the prospect of crossing by the stones.

"Well, Cousin Jane!" Pete lay flat on the grass and propped his head against a tree root. "I wasn't so sure you'd show this morning. It's pretty rough, after all, the old homestead full of foreigners from New York —"

"I suppose you think that's funny."

"No, but I'm trying to keep you from building up a tragedy out of it."

" Thanks! "

" Don't mention it. Mom likes you, by the way."

" Does she? I mean, does she honestly? After the way I tore out of the house? "

" She likes you all the same. Don't be such a worrywart."

" Let me know, Pete, won't you, when you run out of things to criticize about me."

" Oh, don't start getting yourself worked up. Listen, there's something I wanted to ask you. Do you think Uncle Julian would mind if I tried to fix up that old car that's sitting out in the barn at Greenlands? "

" No, I'm sure he wouldn't. Dad puts up this terrible fuss, usually, about any little thing a person wants to do, but he won't care if you want to play around with that old heap of junk. It belonged to a friend of Lonnie's who used to come over and work in the garden sometimes, and it finally fell apart. He left it, and we never got anyone to come and haul it away. What do you want to do with it, Pete? It isn't any good."

" Don't be too sure. I can have some fun playing around with it, anyway. I'm not too dumb about machinery, and I spotted some tools out in the barn. That's one nice thing about living in a place like this — lots of room. In New York we've got about two square feet of back yard, and it's hard on the kids, and summers they've usually been in Vienna or somewhere with Mom and Dad. Do you like poetry? "

" Oh — " Jane felt embarrassed; Pete must have noticed that she was trying to see the name of his book. " It's *The Oxford Book of English Verse*," Pete went on. " It's for my English course, but I like it O.K. Most of the guys I hang out with at school go in for sports — and so do I — but I don't see why that has to exclude everything else, do you? I brought my record player from New York and some dance records, but I've got some LP's of symphonies and what not. I don't dig the serious modern stuff much — poetry, I mean, or music — but I don't know much about it."

" I like *The Oxford Book*, and I've got *The Golden Treasury* too. I kind of like poems if they aren't sloppy. If they're about nature, for instance. Sometimes I like ones that I can't even understand — like some of Yeats or Blake. But I never admitted it before."

" Admitted it! It's O.K. for a girl to like poetry — especially if it isn't sloppy." Pete looked amused.

" What I mean is, I wouldn't do a book report on poetry, for instance. Poetry's kind of private — for me. In English, at school, I'm no good at composition or literature — I usually get about a ' C ' or a ' D ' in my subjects, anyhow."

" Do you study much? "

" No. Only enough to get by."

" How come? "

" Well — it's hard to explain. I like music too, and sometimes I go over to the listening room at the college when there isn't anyone else there. I had piano lessons for a while, but I wasn't any good at it. I tried to paint — Mother used to give art lessons at the college — but I wasn't any good at that. I knew I wouldn't be."

" I don't follow."

" All I mean is, even if I studied I'd never be an all " A " student. Mary Lee is."

" So? "

" So what's the point of knocking myself out? Because it's boring, that's all, and there are lots of things I'm interested in — like tennis. My father's always putting a lot of pressure on me, especially about algebra. I did flunk that. Look — Kai's going to come over! Candy! Sandy! " But the twins had already raced across the stones to meet

Kai who, part way across, stood gazing doubtfully at the biggest gap.

" We'll help you, darling Kai! "

The dog, bewildered by their voices, leaped for the stone on which the twins now stood. Jane, one stone behind, saw children and dog slip into the water in a confused, noisy, splashing heap. She stopped only long to yank off her sneakers before going in after them. There was a brief, mixed-up scramble before she felt ground under her feet; she waded toward the bank, one twin under her arm, the other clutching her around her neck.

" I'll take them. Out of the way, Kai." Pete, who must have crossed the pond while they all floundered in the water, relieved her of the little girls, put them down on the grass, and dodged the spray of drops Kai shook from his coat. " Are you all right, Jane? "

" Of course I am! But, Pete — "

" Comedians! " He was speaking to the twins, who were half laughing, half crying. " Play around here in the sun until you dry off. Mom'll get scared if she sees you coming home with your play suits all wet. If you get into that water again, I'll beat you."

" Did we almost drown, Pete? "

" Kai jumped when we said to."

" We want to come here tomorrow."

" Jane can swim good, Jane, can't you? "

" I'm wetter than you."

" I'm wetter than you! "

" I told Kai to jump first."

They settled down to a low-voiced muttering game with pebbles and pine cones, and Jane turned on Pete, who was stretched out in the grass again.

" Pete! Why didn't you do something? If one of the kids had banged her head on a rock, I could have had a terrible time trying to fish them both out! Why didn't you go in after them too?"

"I didn't want to go in unless I had to." Pete's voice was low, and he didn't look at her as he spoke.

"I never heard anything so silly."

"Oh, stop giving me a hard time!" He sat up. "Look, Jane, I guess I have to explain, but it's something I wasn't going to tell anybody. I'm not supposed to do anything strenuous or I might get sick."

"What?"

"Well, I had rheumatic fever when I was a kid. I was in the hospital with it for a long time, but then I was O.K. I didn't even think about it for years. This spring vacation I went on a faltboat trip; one of the teachers took a bunch of us on the Delaware to learn how to handle white water. After school they were going out west to run some of those big rapids on the Idaho. I chipped in with one of the other guys, and we bought a secondhand Klepper and patched her up. I was going to be in on the Idaho trip; I would have got back east just in time to go abroad with the family. But halfway through the spring-vacation trip I got rheumatic fever again. It was pretty bad; I couldn't go back to school, or even study by myself for a while. That's why I'm working this summer, for make-up exams. And that's why we came to Halford. It's supposed to be peaceful — and restful — and good for me!"

"Oh, Pete!"

"It's so dumb. I'm supposed to loaf around half the time, and I get so fed up with it. Mom watches me like a hawk and keeps on reminding me of what the doctor said. I have to go in to Dr. Jerome's office in Maryville once a week for a checkup. Today I was so tired of hanging around that I came down here and swam and dived and so on. I was going back to the house when I saw you and the kids. I was feeling a little peculiar — I guess maybe I did overdo it — and that's why I didn't go in after you. But, Jane — I would have in a second if I'd seen you having any trouble getting the brats out. I'm on the swimming team at school, and I've done a lot of high diving. I felt like a moron watching you fishing around for the twins. You're a little cold now, aren't you? You don't have as much padding as the kids do. Put this on." He pulled off the white sweater.

"I'm terribly sorry I bawled you out, Pete." Apologies were embarrassing, but it wasn't so hard to make this one through the folds of the sweater as Pete helped her get it over her head.

"How could you know? It must have seemed very peculiar."

"Maybe you'll be perfectly O.K. in no time at all."

He shook his head. "There isn't a chance. If I do everything I'm supposed to this summer — that means not doing much of anything — I might get to go back to school this fall. *Might* — how do you like that? Dr. Jerome says I'll be able to, but he's only trying to cheer me up. He won't promise; he says, 'If nothing unforeseen happens.' I'll probably be a kind of invalid all my life."

"Pete, that's awful. I'm sorry I said once that you didn't have any problems."

"Let's forget it. I told you because I didn't want you to think I was scared of a little water."

"I don't think you're afraid of anything. When I went to get the twins I talked with your mother for a while, and she told me how you got a medal because you risked your life to save someone who was hurt in a ski accident."

"There wasn't any risk involved for a good skier — which to tell you the truth, I am."

"Then why did you get a medal?"

"Oh, they give them away with half a pound of tea in

the Laurentians. Women certainly do an awful lot of talking. Now, listen, Jane, I don't want you to say a word about the ski story or about the rheumatic fever to anyone. Not to your father, not to Mary Lee, not to anybody. Promise?"

"Well, sure, I promise. Of course, you're modest about being a hero — don't laugh, Pete — but why don't you want anyone to know about the rheumatic fever? It isn't your fault."

"The point is, I don't even like to think about it more than I have to. Except for having to take things a little easy, it's not really like being sick. But if people know about it, they get embarrassed. Or they wonder if they've said something tactless. Or they fuss the way my mother does about whether I'm 'overexerting.'"

"I won't say a word to anyone. I think I'm pretty good at keeping promises. Maybe because I'm stubborn. At least, my father says I am — he says I'm obstinate."

"Call it persevering," Pete suggested. "Then it sounds like a good character trait. Eleanor Digges came over one day before she went to Hammond, and she says you're very persevering about learning to keep house."

"I have to be; it's a deal I made with my father. But I'd like to live in a cave, or a tree. Eleanor told me once she *enjoys* scouring pots — especially if they're greasy."

"Mom hates cooking and housework."

"*Does she?*"

"Sure she does. I don't mean she gripes about it. But I suppose if you're married, you have to know how to do things like that, whether you like them or not. Well, you characters," he addressed the twins, who came frolicking up to them, "are you dry? I guess they are."

"I'd better get them back to Greenlands."

"I'll walk up with you. Come on, kids."

" Pete, what do you think of Mary Lee? " asked Jane, as the children ran along the path ahead of them.

" Cute dish. I'd like to get her to school for one of the dances. She'd be a sensation."

" She gets about the best grades at Halford School too. She thinks she could get a scholarship for Swarthmore, probably. That's where she wants to go, but I don't know how her mother would make out without Mary Lee at home."

" She has a tough time, doesn't she? "

" Oh, I don't know about that, Pete. How does she? "

" She seems to be taking care of the little kids a lot of the time, and she said she waits on table in Wilbur Baker's store in the winter, and she has to share her bedroom with — what's her name? Arline — because the house is so small."

" They had a nicer house over near Eleanor's, but it burned down, and Harold Stebbins didn't have any insurance. Wilbur Baker owns the house they live in now, and I guess he doesn't charge a lot of rent. Only, Mary Lee — " And she stopped. Mary Lee always seemed to take it all for granted, that her mother and father weren't practical; everybody said they weren't. Of course, the Stebbinses did have the smallest house in Halford and never went to the lake at all. But why would that matter to a girl who was so popular, and always in a good mood, and so pretty that the college boys had started asking her for dates even though she was barely sixteen! Even if the Stebbins house was always a mess except when Mary Lee kept after things, it was a *nice* family. The Stebbinses all liked one another, and nobody criticized anybody.

" I'm having a much rougher time, Pete."

" Oh? "

" Of course I am! " They had come to the Greenlands

back door, and the twins ran into the house. " I have to work hard too — and nobody cares. But everyone's nice to Mary Lee. Yes, and I wish I had a lot of brothers and sisters the way she does. Pete, you're laughing! "

" Because you're funny. I bet you never even thought about that before — about wanting a lot of little brothers and sisters. Don't get mad, Jane. We haven't had a fight all the way back from the pond."

" Mommy says come in, Pete." The twins appeared behind the screen door. " Jane should come in too, if she's got time."

" Come on," Pete urged. " Let's see if there's some lemonade."

" I have to go back to the cottage and get lunch for Dad."

" O.K. Look, Jane — " he put his hand gently on her arm, where she had pushed the white sweater up above her elbow, " all kidding aside, thanks a lot for taking on the kids. They think you're fabulous. And, how about it, can't we get along together if we put our minds to it? Maybe you could try to overlook the fact that I'm living in your house? "

Jane found she couldn't, for a moment, say anything. Her throat was tight. There was a quivering, sinking sensation somewhere down in the pit of her stomach, and her legs felt queer and weak, as if they might give way under her any minute. Pete was waiting, his long-lashed gray eyes smiling down at her, his hand still light and warm on her arm. " Well — " she said, and swallowed, " I could — I guess I could help you work on that old car in the barn, maybe. If I happen to have the time, and if you show me what to do. I mean, only if you'd like me to, and if I'm not too busy."

" Will you? Great! Come over this afternoon and we'll

94

take a good look at her. I know what — bring your algebra text along and show me what you're supposed to be doing. I finished algebra and started calculus, and I'll help you, but only if you stick with it. All right, kids, I'm coming," he added, for the twins had emerged again and were tugging at him. "So long, Kai; so long, Jane. Hey! Give me back my sweater."

"Is it — is it O.K. if I bring it over this afternoon?"

"Sure. I'll be seeing you."

He vanished into the house, and that was just as well, Jane thought, because she had to get back to the cottage somehow. It was better to be alone if you weren't sure that your legs wouldn't suddenly give way at the knees. She put her hand on Kai's neck and walked slowly as far as the big pine that stood where the path to the cottage made a curve. The branches swept down almost to the ground; she crept underneath, along the smooth ground, inches deep in sweet-smelling needles, and sat down, her back against the rough trunk, her arms around Kai's neck. This was safe, a safe place to think things over.

Because now it was never, never again going to be any use or help at all trying to sell herself the same theory that she had so carefully tried to sell everybody else — that she, Jane Greene, was "different." That she didn't care about boys and dates and looks and clothes. That what she liked most was gardens and tennis and riding her bike. She had believed it herself. She did like all those things and all the other things that meant so much she never talked about them at all. It would be all right, if Pete never, never, never suspected. It was lucky she had told him that awful lie about thinking love poems were sloppy. He would never have any reason to suspect that those were the ones she liked best of all.

Chapter X

JANE stood in the cottage yard, surveyed the scene anxiously, and decided everything looked nice for the supper party. She had already put the yellow cloth on the table close to the house, where she and Dad always ate on fine evenings. Since the table was outside the kitchen door, she could come and go with the food very easily, and things would be hot, at least the ones that were supposed to be. Eleanor said serving things at the right time was half the secret of cooking. Should she have invited Eleanor, she wondered, with a faint twinge of conscience? Yes, probably, but it was too late now. The weather was sultry, but the gnarled apple tree that Dad had wanted to take down because it was so old and close to the cottage would shade the table. The yard looked better, now that Dad had repaired the white picket fence and she had painted it and cut the grass. The two round petunia beds were bright circles of flaming color.

"So that's where you are, Jane!" Mary Lee appeared in the doorway. "I guess you can't hear a bicycle on the drive. I didn't know if anyone was home." She sat down on the kitchen step.

"Hi, Mary Lee."

"I was over at the Larkinses' for butter, and I thought I'd stop here because there's something I want to talk about."

" Well, I have to get supper started because Pete and his mother are coming over. I'm pretty busy because they haven't ever come before. I mean, they've both been here, but not sort of invited and planned and everything. It's just them, not the twins."

" I know. I have to get home because Marion Greene's bringing Candy and Sandy over to our house. You know, Jane, this cottage is kind of cute now. I stuck my head into the study when I came through, and it's a lot nicer, and so is the kitchen. I didn't know it had so many possibilities."

" It's mostly because of things Eleanor showed me. We haven't got to the upstairs yet; it's still pretty crummy."

" But isn't there a lot more furniture? "

" Yes, things from Greenlands. The little sofa in the study and some of the kitchen things and the rugs. Aunt Marion told my father that if he didn't pick out some things from Greenlands for us to use here, she'd hire a truck and have everything brought right over and stuffed into the cottage. She said, ' You're being stiff-necked, Julian Greene, and absolutely ridiculous as well!' "

" What did your father say? "

" Oh, he laughed and said maybe she was right. I was amazed."

" Your father's not so bad. His students like him, and everybody knows he knocks himself out to help them. Are you going to eat outdoors? I think there's going to be a thunderstorm."

" No, there isn't! The weather's been like this for two days." Jane knew she ought to go in and continue with the food preparations and get the table set, but she sat down in one of the striped deck chairs by the petunia beds.

" What are you having to eat, Jane? "

" Jean sent us a huge box from some fancy store in Columbus before she went back to Europe — she probably thinks we're hungry! It's mostly things in little cans or glass jars. There's some wild rice, and I'm going to have curried shrimp and rice for the main dish. I got the shrimp frozen at Hanson's."

" Pete's mad about sea food, isn't he? "

" So's Aunt Marion. Then there were some jars of mushrooms, and I'm going to have a mushroom soufflé. I've never made one, but I borrowed one of Eleanor's cookbooks."

" It sounds pretty ambitious. Pete says you've been working on the car a lot too."

" I'm getting some of the rust spots scoured off."

" The whole thing is one big rust spot. It's an awful lot of work — especially since Pete isn't even sure he can make the car run."

" I don't mind. Pete's been helping me with my algebra. I still don't like it, but the book doesn't confuse me as much as it did."

" When you see Pete, tell him I can go to the barbecue with him next week. Or I can call him and tell him if you forget."

" The barbecue! Did Pete ask you to go to that? I didn't know it was dates, like a dance! Nancy Mead called me about it, and said they were inviting Pete too, because they met him after Meeting for Worship one time while you were still at Young Friends."

" Pete's mother's letting him take the convertible; he told me. That was what I stopped by to tell you, Jane — that you might as well drive out to the Meads' with us. Pete knows you don't date, but that isn't any reason not to go to the barbecue. They're going to have square dancing in the barn, Nancy said. All that Maryville Central gang will be there. I don't know how you'd get out to the Meads', anyhow, if you didn't go with us."

" Did you ever tell Pete I don't go out with boys? Or, I guess what I mean is, do you and he talk about me sometimes, Mary Lee? "

" Sure, sometimes." Mary Lee settled herself on the grass. " Sure we do — just gabbing, the way people do, if we aren't doing anything special. Not that we ever do much of anything special. We went to a movie in Maryville the other night when Pete's mother let him have the car, but usually we just watch TV at my house or listen to records on Pete's player at Greenlands."

" But, Mary Lee — if you talk about me, what does Pete say? I'm kind of curious."

" Let's see if I can remember. Pete said once that the first few times he met you, he didn't know if he was ever going to be able to get along with you at all. He said you had a terrible chip on your shoulder."

" Does he think I still have? "

" Oh, I don't know. He said something the other day about how he seems to get along with you better now, only he still doesn't know when you're going to clam up, or start acting embarrassed or shy — or as if you didn't like him. I said not to pay any attention, because that's the way you've always acted toward everyone you know. Are you mad at me for saying that, Jane? "

" No. Go on. Did Pete say anything else? "

" Oh, he thought you were mature in some ways — like in your job with the twins, and the way you really follow through on some things, like gardening. But he said you're young for your age in other ways, and pretty mixed up — and you kid yourself a lot."

" Kid myself? How? "

Mary Lee wrinkled her forehead in concentration. " Well the gist of that was — now remember, Jane, you're dredging this all up yourself — the whole business about

Greenlands. Pete thinks you don't know the real reason you're making such a production of it. I said once that you act most of the time as if you didn't care about associating with anybody in Halford, and Pete said that what you really thought was that nobody would want to be friends with you unless you lived in the biggest house in Halford."

" How ridiculous! "

" Maybe I haven't even gotten it straight. It was all mixed in with a lot of stuff about how you won't ever compete unless you're sure of winning."

" Of course, I hate not living in Greenlands, but it's for very simple reasons! It's my home, and it's a beautiful house, and my mother was crazy about it, so naturally I am too. Anybody would be." But what Mary Lee said was certainly making her feel a little peculiar, Jane decided. Was it just because Pete had apparently been talking about her in a not very complimentary way — if Mary Lee didn't have it all mixed up? Or was it something else? Caring so much what Pete thought about her had somehow started her caring more than ever about what people in general thought. For one thing, it wasn't so good to have other people tell Pete that she was hard to get along with.

" I guess you are mad now, Jane."

" No, I'm not."

" That's something, anyway. If I'd talked like that once, you would have flared up and said you'd never speak to me again. There's probably nothing to it, anyhow. I'll bet it was Marion Greene who said all that — or said it first, at least."

" She wouldn't say anything mean. She understands the way people feel about things and she doesn't hurt their feelings. And she's always inviting Dad and me over to eat, so that's why I want things to be nice tonight when she comes. She's been terrific to me. I never met anybody so wonderful."

"That's one of the things that's funny about you, Jane, that you don't even know is funny. If you don't like a person — or if you're temporarily mad at somebody — you think there's nothing good about him at all. It's kind of the way you act about your father. Just because he doesn't know exactly how to go about — "

"Go about what?"

"Oh, I don't know exactly. Being sociable and easygoing, I guess. Then about Marion Greene — at first you said you'd never, never even call her 'Aunt Marion,' and now you think she's completely perfect."

"I don't want you to say anything against her, Mary Lee."

"I'm not; don't get me wrong. I think she's fine, myself. One thing about her, though — she likes being efficient and indispensable and running things for people. Don't get excited, Jane, because she knows she's like that. I heard her say so; I don't go around analyzing people!"

"Do you think she runs the twins too much? and Pete?"

"No — just the opposite. She's so mad about them she spoils them a little. Pete's pretty cocky."

"Was Pete at Meeting for Worship yesterday?"

"Yes, he came over to the house for a while afterward."

"He doesn't usually go, but you do every First Day, don't you?"

"Just about."

"Do you ever talk about it with Pete?"

"Oh, some. I know he keeps on harping about how he doesn't want to be a Quaker and be different from other people. He told me that he considered himself an atheist. I don't think he means it, but I know it bothers Marion Greene. I bet your father wishes you'd go."

101

" Pete's almost convinced me he's right. I mean, about religion and God and so on."

" It's too bad you both feel like that. Pete could have gone to one of the Quaker work camps this summer if he'd wanted to. Of course, you'll get to travel sooner or later with your grandmother."

" I doubt it, because I've sort of missed my chance," Jane said; somehow she did not want to tell Mary Lee about Jean's offer to adopt her.

" Larry's mother wrote me the other day, inviting me to come and stay with them at the lake for a couple of weeks."

" Would you like to go? "

" Of course I would. And I've still got enough saved from waiting on table last winter to pay my train fare."

" It would be nice if you could go, with nearly everyone from school there, as well as Larry — " If Mary Lee was so anxious, Jane thought, to go and stay with the Carmichaels, then her seeing quite a lot of Pete didn't mean so much.

" Maybe a little later on I can work it somehow. I hear someone coming."

" That must be Dad, back from the library. I can't stop to talk any more, Mary Lee; I hope you don't mind. When I cook I have to concentrate on it every minute."

Mary Lee got up and laughed. " Of course I don't mind; you've got a lot to do. So long, be seeing you! "

Jane tried not to think too much about the talk with Mary Lee as she set the table and went about her food preparations. When Rachel or Eleanor cooked, they never seemed to have to stop and think what to do first. The bread that she had sliced for garlic bread before Mary Lee came, seemed to have gotten rather dry, but perhaps heating it in the oven with the garlic and butter would improve it. Pete had eaten three slices the last time Aunt Marion had served it. If the oven was hot enough for the soufflé, wouldn't it be too hot for the bread?

Was she planning on too much to eat for a hot summer evening? Was that a mutter of thunder in the distance, or only her imagination? Thank goodness her father, after offering to help, had consented to go into the study and stay put.

A car door slammed, and Aunt Marion came in, calling cheerfully down the hall. " Good evening, Julian, isn't it hot! It was lazy of us to drive over, but I have to go and fetch the children from the Stebbinses' after supper. I thought you might go along, and we'd pay a call on old Professor Rauch and his wife first. Weren't you saying you thought they'd appreciate it? "

" Hi, Jane! " Pete appeared in the doorway.

" Hi! " Jane felt her heart give a suffocating thump. It always happened when she first saw Pete, and then it was all right, usually, but she never could tell when it might happen again, if Pete turned his head or smiled, or even used her name! Dad had taken Aunt Marion around the house, she saw, looking out the back door; they were sitting in the deck chairs by the petunias.

" Mom says, call her in if she can help."

" Oh, no; I don't want her to have to do anything, Pete." Jane peered anxiously into the oven. It was making the kitchen hot, and there were about six things she ought to be doing at once, but she didn't want to ask him to go out into the yard too. Every single minute spent with Pete was terribly important to her.

" I'll put the dressing on the salad." He took the bowl from her. " When we came, I was thinking that the cottage looks like Sleeping Beauty's house, even with the ivy trimmed."

" I was sorry when Dad trimmed it off the roof. He said

it was bad for the shingles, but I'd like it to grow right over, and — and cover up the house." How ridiculous that sounded! She opened the oven again; the soufflé looked as if it was beginning to rise, but obviously the shrimp-and-rice dish had to come out right away; it looked overdone.

"Pete, tell Dad and Aunt Marion to sit down, would you? You too, and I'll bring out the food."

She hurried breathlessly back and forth, wishing they wouldn't all look so sympathetic.

"Let me help carry stuff," Pete urged.

"No, no — it's all right; everything's on now."

"Curried shrimp!" said Aunt Marion. "How lovely! And a soufflé too!"

"It's got French mushrooms in it, Aunt Marion." Nothing was exactly right, Jane thought, tasting despairingly. The soufflé a little gummy, the casserole overdone, the bread dry, the asparagus too soft, the cold tea diluted by melting ice.

There was a rumble in the air; a drop of rain splashed on the yellow cloth.

"Perhaps it will pass over," said Aunt Marion.

Dad looked at the sky, his fork halfway to his mouth. "I'm afraid not. Every summer, around this time in July, we get two or three bad thunderstorms. This looks like the beginning of one of them."

Another raindrop fell on the table. Kai got up from the grass, pushed open the screen door with his nose, and went into the kitchen. Lightning flashed in the distance.

"We'd better move indoors, pup."

"Oh, Daddy, the kitchen's an awful mess, and this table won't go through the hall to the study — it's too big!"

"Then Pete and I'll carry it around the house and take it into the study through the front door. Take the tea glasses off. They might tip over."

"Don't worry, dear," said Aunt Marion. Rain began to fall more heavily. "I'll help you carry the food through the house so it won't get wet."

"Everything's ruined already," wailed Jane, and grabbed the casserole. The next few minutes, she decided, as they all worked feverishly to reassemble the meal in the study, were just like one of those nightmares in which there was something desperately urgent that had to be done, not enough time to do it, and everything going wrong the minute it was touched!

When at last they sat down again, she found herself wishing that the food had come out worse, because then, at least, it might have been so awful that it could have treated as a joke. At any rate, dessert would be all right, she hoped!

Out in the hot, cluttered kitchen, darkened by the rain streaming down the windows, she looked frantically for the little nest of dessert bowls — were there four to match? There should be, but maybe she had used one or two to store something in the refrigerator.

"Look, gal," said Pete, who had followed her in from the study, "stop running around a minute and listen."

"Oh, here are the bowls for the strawberries! But I wanted to open one of the boxes of fancy cookies from Jean to go with them, and I can't remember where they are!"

"Don't panic." Pete pulled open a couple of cupboard doors. "I found them, a whole stack of goodies. How about these? They're some kind of chocolate wafer."

"Or the ones with walnuts? Pete, you decide."

"If you can't relax when you do something like this, then the people you're feeding can't help worrying about you."

"I — I know you're right."

"You do? Boy, that gives me a turn. I expected you to snap at me. The rain was bad luck enough to throw anyone."

Carefully Jane arranged the four little bowls of berries on the round black tray. "As far as snapping at people goes — well, a person can change sometimes."

"Most people don't think they need to. Take me, for instance. I'm practically perfect."

"Your mother thinks you are."

Pete laughed. "Good for you! You're getting harder to tease, Jane. What's this? More tea? I'll carry it in."

Jane noticed gratefully when she came into the study that Dad had lighted the two candles on the mantel. The room *was* rather pretty! With the candles burning, the whole scene looked a little more the way she had hoped it would — rather glamorous!

"Wonderful strawberries, Janey, exactly right to finish a summer meal!" A little later, Aunt Marion put down her spoon. "But we should be on our way to Halford, Julian, if we want to fit in a call on the Rauchs. I don't want to leave the twins at the Stebbinses' too long past their usual bedtime. Will you go along, Pete?"

"No, I'll stay and help Jane with the dishes and walk back to Greenlands afterward. The rain's dying down already."

It didn't *mean* anything, not a thing, Jane assured herself when the car had driven off, and she was mechanically stacking the dirty plates. The reason Pete hadn't gone along was because he didn't want to get involved in the call on the elderly Rauchs, even if it would have given him a chance to see Mary Lee afterward. Or else he thought he ought to help with the dishes. She felt the copper boiler; plenty of hot water. It *was* nice, being alone in the cottage with Pete — just as if —

"This is the last of the stuff from the study, Jane." Pete put down a tray. "What now?"

"Actually, there's nothing much to do till it's time to dry the silver. Sit down and — and talk awhile, why don't you?"

"No, I know what. Where's that iron you were telling me about, that sends out sparks? I brought along my pocket tool kit. I'm afraid if Uncle Julian tampers with it, he'll burn down the cottage."

Jane got the iron out, and caught a glimpse of her algebra textbook lying on the same shelf. She hoped the iron would occupy Pete so he wouldn't think to ask her about the algebra. She hadn't done any for two days.

"What's this barbecue thing going to be like, Jane?"

"Oh, the Meads have it every summer. There's square dancing and regular dancing in their barn — it's huge. And a bonfire in the orchard, with pork sandwiches on rolls and barbecue sauce, and roasting ears."

"Where'd you get this iron, Jane? It's like something from Noah's ark."

"It's an extra one Eleanor Digges had and gave me so we wouldn't have to buy one."

"That was nice of her."

"Sure it was, but of course she likes to do things for us. She *is* boring, Pete."

"There, now you're in business again." Pete put down the iron and picked up a dish towel. "About Eleanor — she isn't as simple-minded as you think she is. She likes to chatter — so what? Also, she's smart enough to know you think she's boring. So that panics her, and she chatters more. Mom likes Eleanor; she says she's really unegotistical. You're awfully intolerant about her."

Jane scrubbed fiercely at the soufflé dish. Pete had no way of knowing, of course, that criticism from him left her much more shattered-feeling than criticism from anybody else in the world.

"The stuff that's in the drainer can stand, Pete." She hoped her voice didn't sound hurt and shaky.

"O.K. I suppose I should be thinking about getting back, but let's do the algebra first. How'd you make out with that last batch of equations?"

"I didn't do them all, Pete. As a matter of fact, I didn't do any of them yet."

"How come? Look, you've been stalling more and more on this algebra business."

"I've been busy the last couple of days."

"I know you've got a lot to do, but this is something you can't goof off on indefinitely. You're never even going to graduate if you can't pass a simple math requirement, are you?"

"I don't care if I ever graduate or not."

"Of course you care. Don't be silly. You'll be going to college."

"No, I won't. I won't have a good enough average to get in anywhere."

"Yes, you will, because you've got two years left to pull it up, so stop talking foolishness. I like to have you help me with the car, but don't you think you'd better spend less time on it? Jane! Are you *crying?*"

"No!" Jane ran into the study, closing the door behind her, but in a moment she heard Pete's footsteps in the hall. He didn't have sense enough to let a person alone who wanted to be alone. She buried her face in a sofa pillow, but she knew Pete was standing beside her.

"What's the matter? Was it something I said?"

"Oh, go away!" What did Pete think could possibly be making her cry, Jane wondered, if it wasn't something he had said! Hadn't he wanted her to help with the car? It

108

had been something to look forward to every day, the first thing she thought of when she woke up mornings — that sense of companionship that came from working under Pete's directions. It wasn't ever necessary to say much of anything, because he had always seemed perfectly contented to do most of the talking, telling her all about school and his friends, who all sounded so wonderful! Like Mario Falcone, who had his own boat, and he and Pete sailed it in races —

"Hey, Jane!" Pete shook her shoulder gently. "What is it — was I too rough about the algebra, or what? Or did you think I don't appreciate your working on the car? I know it's dull for you because you don't care about the mechanical part, but it's nice to have somebody helping — makes it a lot more fun!"

"It's O.K. I've stopped crying. I — I don't know exactly what's the matter."

"Maybe it still sort of aggravates you, having us around, because we're living in your house. But, Jane, we can't help existing! After all, if my dad hadn't taken the job, somebody else would have. And whoever else took it would probably have rented Greenlands for the summer too."

"No, it wouldn't have been like that. Dad was the next in line for the job, Pete."

"Uncle Julian! I never thought of that! It would have solved a lot of problems, wouldn't it? I'm sorry, Jane. You never said anything, and it never occurred to me. Naturally it upsets you to think you were that close. Well, maybe my pop won't be staying."

"Oh, Pete!" Jane sat up. "I shouldn't have said anything. Your mother's been wonderful about the house. I'm not crying, and I didn't cry — much!"

"That's good!"

"You're right about the algebra. I could find time to

109

work on it if I wanted to. But it's good of you to help me with it."

"Yes, I'm bighearted!" Pete laughed. "Well, I'll be moving along, since things seem to have cleared up all around. See you tomorrow."

"It was nice of you and your mother to come over, I mean, to take a chance on my cooking."

Pete laughed again. "I *like* coming over. I *like* having you around. A person gets his money's worth of excitement, wondering what you're going to do or say next! And thanks for having us."

Jane watched him disappear, whistling, along the footpath. "Oh, Kai — I feel tired!" She scooped up a few remaining chocolate wafers from the dish and fed them to Kai, one by one. "But I feel much better too!"

Chapter XI

THE CAR slid softly through the warm summer twilight. Pete was driving very slowly, and Jane, who had been watching the first golden flashes of the fireflies in the cornfields, turned her head to look at him. Mary Lee, between them, had put her head back against the seat and her eyes were closed. So it was safe to look at Pete's profile and his hands on the wheel.

But it wasn't much use pretending that there were only the two of them in the car. For one thing, Mary Lee was wearing perfume. It was a nice smell, but it blotted out the scent of grass and clover from the fields. She was looking even prettier than usual. She had on a wide red skirt, a low-necked, frilly white blouse, a ribbon in her hair. Her skin was a little tanned, and looked warm and glowing.

"Where do I turn off, Jane? You'll have to tell me, since old Mary Lee here seems to have flicked out on us."

Mary Lee opened her eyes and smiled at him. "I'm conscious. It's the next left, Pete, and then you come to the Meads' in half a mile. We're almost there, in fact."

If only they weren't! thought Jane. Because she had the "party feeling" already, her muscles tight, the palms of her hands moist and cold. The older everyone got, the worse parties were for her, because people paired off more and more. It wasn't so bad when they were all kids. When Mother had a birthday party for her at Greenlands, that was wonderful, because Mother always enjoyed herself so much that somehow everybody always had a wonderful time. Those parties had always started with musical chairs, Mother playing on the old, square rosewood piano in the living room and laughing over her shoulder at the running, excited children. Thinking of it, Jane could almost feel again the pigtails she used to wear, flopping up and down on her shoulders. Dad had asked her tonight, before she left, why she didn't get her hair cut in Maryville instead of hacking away at it herself with a pair of scissors. It must look pretty bad, for Daddy to notice it! What was the use of trying when a person had hair that was straight *and* wispy *and* sandy-colored?

"Here we are, Pete!" Mary Lee sat up, looking excited. "Turn in that driveway and go past the house; they'll be out in the orchard near the barn, where the outdoor fireplace is."

"Hi, you all!" Nancy Mead came bounding up to the car as Pete brought it to a stop. "Hop out and come on over to the fire. Everybody else is here. Marsh Vickers brought his guitar, and we're singing; it's great! He's going to call for us when the trio gets here. We're going to dance a couple of sets and come back out here and eat and then dance some more. Mary Lee, what a sensational outfit! "

Jane saw that Pete liked the look of the orchard scene, and no wonder! It was lovely! The fire had been allowed to get very low, but it was bright enough to light up the green leaves and throw a rosy glow on the faces of everyone sprawled around it.

The boys were in jeans, but most of the girls were dressed more or less like Mary Lee. Oh, if only she had worn jeans herself, instead of the seersucker skirt! Everybody was used to seeing her in jeans except in school or Meeting. Not dressing up showed she didn't care about boys. If only she could be back in the cottage kitchen right this minute, doing the supper dishes, with Kai snoozing on the floor and the crickets chirping outside!

" Hey, dopey! " Pete, returning from the circuit of introductions, sat down on the grass and yanked her down beside him. " What are you standing there like a log on a log for? "

Thank goodness for that! It solved the problem of picking a place in the circle to sit down. There was a huge old stump behind them; she wedged her back against it and felt safer. How wonderful to know she would be sitting next to Pete for the singing! She hadn't dared to count on that.

" Look, Jane." He pointed to the open barn door, outlined by the lights inside against the dark bulk of the building. " As I live and breathe, a parallelogram! But I shouldn't make any mathematical allusions; you might burst into tears."

" I don't mind geometry, Pete. Geometry's logical — and — and so am I."

" Logical? Well, possibly, in a screwball kind of way. But I guess that's the most you expect of girls."

" What's that? " Mary Lee was settling herself, as a matter of course, on Pete's other side.

" A little logic and slightly twisted."

" Well, that's all right," said Mary Lee comfortably.

" What we were really talking about was Jane and algebra. It looked like a close decision for a while, but now I think she's got it licked."

Marsh's guitar struck up. How sweet the voices sounded, and the plunk, plunk of the music! She was so close to Pete that she could feel his chest move. A round moon rose as they sang, freed itself from the apple trees, and floated, lightly as a bubble, up into the clear, starlit air. It was like a spell, Jane thought, seeing how the boys and girls around the circle moved gently closer together, becoming pairs. Oh, her heart felt as large as the moon!

" He asked me would I marry him and be his sweet wife,
    And we would live together all of our life."

Pete leaned back as the voices rang out; he put one arm around Mary Lee's shoulders, the other, lightly, around Jane's.

" Oh —— oh —— kisses sweeter than wine,
    Oh —— oh —— kisses sweeter than wine! "

" Hey, listen! " called Billy, as the chorus died away. The sound of a violin being tuned came from the barn, and Jane felt each tiny twang vibrate through her. " There's the trio! " Billy said. " On your feet, loafers; let's go and dance! " He threw a piece of kindling on the fire, and the embers blazed up. " How about it, Mary Lee? " he asked, and pulled her to her feet. " You promised me the first set when school broke up."

" Sure I did, Billy. I remember! " Mary Lee smiled at him, brushed twigs from her pretty skirt, and let him take her hand and lead her toward the barn. Jane watched them, while the others, laughing, stretching, yawning, got up and began to follow. Even though Mary Lee didn't care

113

about Billy, who was younger than she was, and kiddish for his age anyway, she was always nice enough to him to keep him hopeful. Jane jumped up. It would be awful if Pete thought, even for a minute, that she was hanging around after the others had gone, to be with him — or anything like that!

"Better move along, I guess." Pete got to his feet and looked around him at the moonlit orchard. "It's like a poem here now, Jane, isn't it?"

"Oh, yes! And I like the way trees are different at night — more — more real or something."

"Hey!" yelled Nancy from the barn. "Come on in, you two! We're making up the sets!"

"Coming!" called Pete.

The sets were all ready, Jane saw, except for two places in the last one, and the six people in it claimed her and Pete to make it up. Mary Lee and Billy were 'way over at the other end of the room. So it was natural for Pete to be her partner. It was a marvelous party so far! If only Pete would not overdo it and dance all the time — but it was probably more tactful not to bring it up yet.

"O.K.!" shouted Marsh. "Sets in order, ladies and gents! We're going to start with 'Buffalo Boys'!"

"Here we go!" Pete smiled down at her. "I've hardly ever done this, Jane. I hope I don't gum up the set. You'll have to watch and shove me through it."

"Oh, this one's easy, and Marsh is a wonderful caller."

The music struck up. "Bow to your corners!" shouted Marsh. "Bow to your partners! All join hands, circle once around, and an *allemande* to your left!"

They were caught up into the bright, swinging, twanging rhythm of the music; everything was blended yet distinct: Nancy Mead's hot, happy face; Pete's dark head always in sight, even when the figure of the dance separated them; his handclasp as they passed in the grand right and left — oh, and the music! It was a little, sparkling stream, running through her veins! Pete was dancing marvelously and hardly needed any prompting at all from the others. But, then, Pete could do anything!

Was the set really over? It seemed impossible, but the music had stopped, and Pete set her down after a final twirl that lifted her off her feet. " That was fun! " he said. " You're as light to swing as a grasshopper, Jane! "

" Big circle, everybody! " called Marsh. " We're going to do a Grand Chain. Ladies, make the most of the gent you get when the music stops, because you're stuck with him! "

That meant not dancing with Pete any more — unless he asked her later on. He probably would, once at least. Unless by some chance the Grand Chain Around brought them together — no, the music was stopping already and she was clasping Billy Mead's pudgy hand. Well, that was better than if it had been one of the older boys she hardly knew. Billy wouldn't mind, especially, getting her for a set.

" Having a good time, Jane? "

" Oh, yes, Billy; it's a sensational party! " Pete, two sets away, had Betty Meier for a partner, and Betty was looking terribly pleased.

" Sets in order! ' Dig for the Oyster, Dive for the Clam.' "

When the dance was over, Billy's round face looked ready to melt.

" Let's go have some pop, Jane; there's a lot in an ice tub over in the corner."

Everyone else had had the same idea and was gathered around the tub. They were listening to Pete, who was perched on a sawhorse and looking excited. He was talking about sports. It didn't sound like bragging; Pete didn't brag. The girls were eating it up, but the boys looked sulky. Mary Lee, sitting on a bale of straw, her wide skirts flowing over it, was egging Pete on. It was probably to show off that she knew him well, Jane decided.

"I like Western skiing best, but not the resort kind of place where the snow bunnies go. Last Christmas vacation a bunch of us from school went out to Colorado. We used to take our gear and start out around three o'clock in the morning and climb six hours to the top of the mountain. No chair lifts or tows!"

"You've skied a lot in Europe too, haven't you, Pete?" Mary Lee asked.

"Mountain-climbing, mostly, because we usually go over summers, for a few weeks, anyway. My mother's got a relative married to an Austrian — some kind of baron. He's got a castle in the Tirol — a crazy place — where we stay, and Uncle Otto takes me on some of the big climbs with him."

Jane dug her nails into the palms of her hands. If Pete would only stop talking now — if only he would realize that the boys were hating every word of it!

"Have a cigarette, Pete," Johnny Meier interrupted him. That was typical of Johnny, who liked to brag about smoking two packs a day, though nobody believed him.

"No, thanks."

"Go on, Pete; tell us some more about the climbing." Betty Meier glared at her brother.

"What's the matter?" said Johnny, and struck a match. "Doesn't anybody smoke at prep school? Or is it because you're a Quaker and little Quaker boys never do anything they shouldn't?"

Pete got off the sawhorse. "When I want you or anybody to talk about Quaker boys or prep schools, I'll let you know."

"And Quaker boys don't burn down barns." Nancy Mead sounded furious. "For heaven's sake, Johnny, be careful, with all this hay and straw around. Put the cigarette out, you idiot; our dairy herd's in the other side of this barn."

Johnny began to chin himself on a low beam. "How about this, Pete? Did they teach you to do this in *Zürich?*" He imitated Pete's way of pronouncing the word.

That started all the boys off doing silly things. They were all chinning themselves, doing push-ups, wrestling on the floor, needling Pete, trying to draw the girls' attention to themselves.

"I dare you to do this, Pete!" Harry Douglas ran up a ladder and jumped off it, landing with a thud that shook the floor. A couple of the girls screamed.

"There's no special point to it," said Pete. He was leaning against the wall, and spoke in a cool, superior voice. "However — " He ran up the ladder and jumped down, landing lightly with his knees bent. "Skiing technique!" he said. "You have to learn it for jumping."

Milt Weatherbee had just succeeded in pinning Benny Sellers' shoulders to the floor, and he looked up at Pete. "Take you on!" he said.

Jane took a deep breath and wished she didn't feel so shaky. "I have to talk to you a minute, Pete."

He gave her a cross look. "Later." And he moved toward Milt.

"I absolutely have to talk to you this minute, Pete, about something private and very important."

"Later, I said!" He looked really angry — and, of course, it was all very conspicuous, with everyone wondering what it was all about. Then the music started, and Billy and Nancy herded everyone back to the dance floor. Milt looked relieved. Pete said something in a low voice to

Mary Lee, then turned and pulled Jane into a dusty corner shielded by some bales of straw.

"Look, Jane, let's get this over. I know what's eating you, and you're wasting your time."

"Pete, I'm sorry, but I had to say something. Please don't get into any wrestling matches — and I think you ought to rest a while before you dance any more."

"Once and for all, Jane, I want to decide for myself how much I feel like doing. I don't want you to start mixing yourself up in it. I'm sorry you ever found out anything about my being sick. It's bad enough having Mother harp away about the whole situation. And let's not have any more of these mystery conferences, either. Do you want people jumping to the conclusion that there's something wrong, or that I'm afraid to do anything these guys can do?"

"Oh, Pete, nobody could possibly think that! You're being awfully unfair —"

But Pete had walked off. So that was that, Jane thought. Probably Pete would be even more reckless because she had annoyed him. Slowly she moved out of the protecting corner. The dance was a waltz — was anybody going to ask her? No, apparently not. She didn't really know how to dance anything but square dances. Some of the boys were clustering around the barn door, not dancing, so she could pretend she wanted another drink and sit with the other girls who hadn't been asked. Pete was waltzing with Mary Lee, who was singing softly and looking up at him as she danced. They stayed together when the next dance began, and Jane was now the only girl without a partner. Billy Mead wasn't in the barn — he had probably gone to the house to help his mother and father bring the food out to the orchard — and the numbers were even.

Jane slipped out of the barn door and walked back to the

118

fire, which was now only a faint, red glow. She wouldn't be so conspicuous here, and maybe nobody would notice that she hadn't been dancing — and she could think about how lovely it had been during the singing. She stepped quickly behind a tree, for she saw, outlined against the light coming from the barn door, the figures of Pete and Mary Lee walking toward the fire. The music was still playing. Were they — could they be looking for her?

"Everyone's going to notice we're gone, Pete." Mary Lee's voice came softly but clearly over the few yards of distance.

"What difference does it make if they do?"

"By the way, what did Jane want to talk to you about, back in the barn?"

"Oh, nothing, a bee in her bonnet. Forget it. Look, the fire's almost out, but you can see by the moonlight. Mary Lee — "

A puff of pearl-gray cloud slid across the moon, but not before Jane had seen Mary Lee lift her head suddenly and Pete bend his to kiss her. They had not moved apart when, a few seconds later, the cloud had passed.

Jane leaned back dizzily for support against the rough bark of the tree under which she stood. Now the important thing was to be sensible. Yes — sensible and calm, though her heart was pounding and her breath coming in short, quick gasps as if there wasn't enough air. The sensible thing was to go away, very quickly and secretly and quietly, so that no one could see her and stop her. She would be sensible and calm as soon as she was safely away from the orchard, and the last, expiring glow of the fire, and the two figures silent in each other's arms.

The first part of the escape was easy enough, slipping from tree to tree, her feet soundless on the grass, till she got to the short drive that led to the road. Here she had to wait so as not to be seen by Billy and his parents, who came out of the house carrying baskets and bags.

Now she was safe at last on the road. The moon was higher in the sky now, cold, small, pale, compared to its appearance when it rose, and the road looked hard and pale in its light. Jane set off; even by taking the cross-country way it would be a long time before she was home and in bed.

There were mosquitoes on this road. There hadn't been any in the orchard; perhaps the fire had kept them away. The orchard — she stopped to listen. The sound of music that had pursued her down the drive and along the road had faded away in the quiet night air. It was easier to think without the sound of the music.

Imagine — just imagine — having been dumb enough to think, even for a minute, that Pete maybe took her seriously as a girl, or even as a person. She had talked herself into thinking that he and Mary Lee were sort of passing the time together — that it didn't mean anything. After all, people liked having Mary Lee around even when there wasn't any romance involved, because she was fun to be with.

Jane paused and looked around; here was the little path through the Meiers' wood lot that began the cross-country way home. Nobody would notice she had left the barbecue, and nobody would be able to find her anyway except on foot, and she had a head start. The path was dark and difficult because the trees met overhead and little moonlight came through.

What about Larry Carmichael? Didn't Mary Lee care about him any more? Nice, lanky Larry with his shock of red hair and his good-natured, crooked smile? He was the most popular boy at school, as Mary Lee was the most popular girl. Had Mary Lee said anything to Pete about

Larry? What Jane had seen in the orchard was making her feel bad in a special way.

She began to walk faster as she came out of the woods to open fields. How did people learn to live with something awful? Especially without religion to help. Mother had talked about religion — at the end. She had never been interested in Halford Meeting the way Dad and Eleanor were; she got bored sometimes with things like being on the supper committee. But the last time, when she had come home to Greenlands from the Maryville hospital, then Mother had talked about religion. She had brought it up herself one day when she was feeling a little bit better, and the nurse had gone downstairs for a cup of coffee, and she was sitting up in bed wearing her pink, quilted jacket, with her hair in braids.

"Do you know, Janey, I've been wanting to tell you something, and that is, I'm glad, terribly glad now, that I'm a Friend. I wish I'd been a better one — but I've always been excited about so many other things. But it's being a Friend that's seeing me through now. Remember that. Oh, dear, what a pair you and Daddy will be! But you'll have the Meeting, both of you — and poor Jean doesn't have anything like that."

Jane hadn't known what to answer, because it was all so dreadful, with Daddy shut up in his study except when he was sitting with Mother, and Eleanor haunting the house and crying in corners. It *was* terribly hard to talk about anything really personal with somebody, even though it might — might be the last time. But why, Jane wondered, was she thinking about it now? There didn't seem to be any line of thought that didn't hurt one way or another.

She made a circuit to avoid passing Stepping Stones, and, when she reached the cottage, stood and stared at it, dazed. It was not dark and quiet and peaceful the way she had imagined it would be, with herself slipping up the narrow stairs to her room. The lights were on and the door was open.

"Jane, is that you?" Her father burst out of the study. "Where on earth — they called from the Meads' to ask if you were here, a good hour and a half ago!"

"I walked home."

"All that way, and without saying anything? They've been out scouring the countryside — the party's spoiled. I just called Eleanor to ask her to lend me the car so I could go and look."

"I came the cross-country way, through the Meiers' lot and over the fields."

"But, why?"

"I — I didn't feel like staying."

"But to leave without a word —"

"I didn't see what business it was of anybody's." Jane knew her voice sounded hateful.

"Whatever got into you, you ought to have thought of other people for once! Rose Mead's been out of her mind with worry, feeling responsible, and wondering if you were lost or drowned or run over — almost anything could have happened! Jane, I thought you were making progress this summer, learning to get along with people. But something like this makes me feel hopeless. I'll go call the farm and Eleanor. You'd better have something to eat — I suppose you're exhausted — and go straight to bed!"

Jane went directly upstairs, and dropping down on the bed without taking her clothes off, fell instantly asleep.

Chapter XII

THE PERSISTENT ringing of the cottage telephone woke Jane, who saw with surprise that the sun was high. It must be well on in the morning. She hurried downstairs; only Kai was in the study, and the clock on the desk said almost eleven. She picked up the receiver and said, " Hello," hesitantly.

" Hi, Jane! "

" Oh, Billy Baker! " She felt relieved. " I overslept; I was up late on account — on account of the barbecue at Meads'. But I wasn't supposed to meet you for tennis till twelve, was I? "

" That's what I called up about, to say never mind."

" Never mind! Why? "

" Ed's back from the lake; he got here yesterday. I'm going over to the courts with him; he says he'll give me a lesson every day till the fall semester starts."

" I didn't even know Ed was coming back! Didn't he say anything about calling me or coaching me? "

" Nope — he probably didn't think of it yet. Come on down to the courts and watch my lesson if you want to, Jane."

" *Thanks*, Billy! " Jane hung up the receiver, and suddenly aware of a ravenous hunger, went to the kitchen. After all the time and effort she'd spent on Billy's tennis!

Well, he had had his last session with her! And Ed would rather coach a little boy than her!

A bowl on the table showed that her father had breakfasted on cold cereal and milk. Was he still terribly angry with her about last night? There was the prospect, too, of calling Nancy and Billy's mother to apologize for running away. What would Pete have to say about that? Would he be sarcastic, or tease her? Or was he still furious with her?

The strange thing was, Jane decided as she began to eat the eggs she had hastily scrambled, that she felt somehow calm, as if something had been settled, something inside her had relaxed.

Putting the breakfast dishes to soak, she dressed and started for Greenlands. She had promised yesterday to come and work on the car around ten. She tried to analyze her new feeling as she walked along the footpath. It wasn't that she had stopped caring desperately about Pete — no such luck! It wasn't that she didn't still mind terribly having seen him kiss Mary Lee. She felt now as if she was going to learn to — to cope with it somehow, and the wild, whirling bitterness and misery of the walk back in the moonlight seemed far away and dreamlike.

Pete was not in the barn. He was not in the house — nor was anyone else. Jane looked and called, then stepped out the front door just as Marion Greene drove up.

" Hi! " Jane ran down to open the car door, puzzled by the fact that her aunt greeted her as if hardly recognizing her, walked slowly up the steps and into the house, and, once in the hall, paused and looked about her as if she was dazed.

" I've just come from the hospital."

" What? "

" Oh, dear, you haven't heard a thing about it, Jane. I

should have called the cottage, but it's all been such a rush and confusion. Pete wasn't well early this morning, and I took him in to Maryville."

" Oh, Aunt Marion! The rheumatic fever thing again? "

" Yes, but not serious. At least, I hope not." She looked helplessly around her.

" Come into the kitchen, Aunt Marion, and let me get you some tea and a sandwich or something. I bet you haven't eaten anything today."

" I don't think I have." Aunt Marion followed Jane obediently to the kitchen and sat down. " The Larkinses have been inviting the twins to come and spend a morning at the farm; you know how they adore watching the cows. So I sent Rachel over with them when I saw that something was wrong with Pete."

" Tell me about him." Jane put the tea water on to boil. Her hand felt shaky. " Isn't it — isn't it serious if he has to be in the hospital? "

" Not necessarily. When he admitted, finally, this morning that he didn't feel all right, I called Dr. Jerome. He said to bring him in to Maryville for a general checkup and a complete rest, and to try a new treatment he thinks might help. Oh, I wish Pete's father were here — or our doctor back in New York, who's known us all for years."

" Everyone in Halford goes to Dr. Jerome, and everyone says he's wonderful. It's bound to be O.K. Probably the new treatment will make Pete completely well."

" It's been such a comfort to me, Jane, your knowing about this all along. Pete's such a ridiculous young ostrich about not telling people. I know it's made you patient with some of his moods, and I know you've tried to stop him from overdoing things. He gets terribly annoyed with me when I try."

" He got terribly annoyed with me last night when I

tried! I'll make you a cheese sandwich while the tea's steeping."

"When I think of all the times I've advised people not to get excited and miserable about some calamity that may never happen! Of course, it's easier to advise other people not to borrow trouble than it is to be sensible yourself."

When she had eaten the sandwich and drunk the tea, she poured herself a second cup and said, " That's better! " and smiled at Jane. "Don't look at me so anxiously, dear; I'm all right, and Pete will be too."

"Shall I make you another sandwich, Aunt Marion? "

"No, dear. Sit down and have some tea yourself, and tell me if you're all right. Pete came back from the barbecue very disturbed and said you had left the party — no one knew why — and everyone had been driving around the countryside looking for you. Some time later your father called to say you were home. What was the trouble? "

"It — it was a couple of things."

"Pete told me he'd been very cross with you for trying to warn him to take things easy. But he couldn't imagine, he said, that that was enough to make you run off — "

"I feel awfully embarrassed about it now."

"Mary Lee said she didn't know what the matter could have been either, when I called her today."

"Oh — does Mary Lee know about Pete? "

"Yes. He asked me to call her and explain. They'd been planning to do something together today. She was concerned, poor girl, and blamed herself, though of course she'd never known anything before about Pete's being sick. She's going to go in with me this afternoon to see him. Honey, what's the matter? "

"Nothing, Aunt Marion."

"Nothing? But you look so unhappy, Jane. Is it — is it Pete's having asked for Mary Lee rather than — rather than for you, to come to Maryville? "

"Why should he ask for me?"

"Now that the subject has come up, I want to talk to you about something — this whole business of your not taking any interest in your appearance. And the way you're so extremely — how shall I put it — unflirtatious with Pete, and I suppose with other boys."

"Aunt Marion!"

"Well?"

"You're talking as if — as if I was just like anybody else. I mean — like any other girl."

"For goodness' sake, aren't you?"

"No, I'm not. You know I'm not. Because other girls are pretty, or — or anyway, not bad-looking. They aren't — homely."

"Oh, my dear!" Was it possible that Aunt Marion was *laughing?* "Honey, I'm sorry. I shouldn't laugh, but I'm staggered, honestly I am. Is that what you've been brooding about? I suspected something or other along those lines, but I never realized you were exaggerating so much!"

"Exaggerating?"

"Why, of course! Jane, lamb, you could be really attractive. But first you'd have to believe in the possibility — that's half the battle. And secondly, you'd have to work at it."

"Work at it how?"

"Well, start with fundamentals. Your weight, for instance. I think you've started to gain a little lately anyway, haven't you? But about ten pounds more would do wonders for your face and figure. I'll make you out a diet if you let me, and if you promise to stick to it. Luckily, Julian could use some extra weight too, so you won't have to cook separately for yourself. And let your hair grow, Jane. We'll curl it, fluff it out around your face, and perhaps use something on it to bring out glints — a vinegar rinse might be

127

enough. Then we'll see about some clothes, and some very simple make-up. I've watched you making the worst of yourself, dear, and I've wondered why."

" Because it all seemed so hopeless — "

" Oh, nonsense! I suppose you've told yourself that you don't care about all the things that make life so much fun for a pretty girl."

" I guess so."

" And did you convince yourself? "

" Not lately — I mean, not completely. But it all sounds as if I was kind of squirrely."

" Maybe squirrely, but it's human. I think I understand something about it, because I went through the same thing myself at about your age. Instead of going in for tennis, I persuaded myself that nothing was important to me except being head of my class at school. I'm not saying that studies don't matter — and sports too — but only as one part of life. Once you get started, Jane, you can be much prettier than I've ever been. There's nothing wrong with your features or your figure — and they'll both improve as you mature over the next few years."

" Aunt Marion, I *never* think about your looks — No, I don't mean that! It sounds awful! What I mean is, I like the way you look — because it's you! "

" Thank you, honey! But even in my younger days, you know, I never exactly stopped the traffic. I had to learn to make the most of my looks — and of my lack of looks — and to live with it. Your Uncle Charles fell in love with me anyway, and I'm having a wonderful life! But I suppose, Jane, that there aren't many days that go by that it doesn't cross my mind, fleetingly at least. I remember that I'm not pretty — and I mind, just a little! It's the way women are, I suppose."

" But everyone likes you so much, Aunt Marion. I know

Daddy wishes I would grow up to be like you."

" Nobody ever did like me until I learned to like myself."

" What? "

" They were right; I wasn't worth liking. I can't explain what I mean unless I talk about religion, and you'll shy like a startled fawn if I do that."

" I don't mind, if you want to, Aunt Marion."

" All right, then. To begin with, people are complicated. We have a lot of layers, physical, spiritual, psychological; we have needs and possibilities that are intertwined and that we're aware of only in the dimmest way, most of the time. Things crop up in the form of problems that make people unhappy, and they don't quite understand why. Now if you work at being a good Quaker or a good anything — really live that way — then you have some hope of getting to know yourself. For one thing, you begin to develop a sense of proportion because you're living with eternity in mind. You learn how to change some of the things that are bad about yourself, and to face and control some of the others, so that you don't hurt other people. You can forget yourself and really reach out. When your own ego, your own personality, isn't the center of your universe, the way is cleared for contacts with other people, loving them and understanding them. That's how you get love and understanding back — but you can't do it on a bargain basis. You know that you fall short of what you'd like to be, of course, and that you always will, so you stop expecting others to measure up to some impossible standard you set. I'm condensing a lot of this, Jane, and I don't know if you follow what I'm saying? "

" Some of it I do. You think I criticize an awful lot, for one thing, don't you, Aunt Marion? "

" Sometimes, dear. You expect life to be ' fair,' I think. Well, ultimately it is — at least I believe so — but not in our limited human terms. There are a lot of mysteries in the universe. But the kind of demands, Jane, that you make on life and people, as if you had a right to them, is a following of your own will. As a Quaker, I believe that there is something of God in all men, and that we can know his will for us, if we want to. I suppose that, like Pete, you're going through a time of doubt as to whether there is anything in the whole thing at all — any reality. You will have to decide for yourself. But meantime — "

"What about meantime? What do I have to do? "

"Well, you have to love without feeling a right to a return. Or, at least, you mustn't demand a return on your terms. You have to love spontaneously — as you do Kai, for instance, when you don't stop to measure what return you're getting. Wilbur Baker does it. It's not easy, of course; it's probably the hardest thing in the world to learn. If you don't love God, and people, and doing your duty spontaneously, you have to do it by an act of will. You have to find out the right ways, and act in the right ways, and hope that the real feeling will follow."

"It sounds impossible, Aunt Marion."

"No — because God helps, or we couldn't do it at all. What does seem really 'unfair' is that certain people seem to have been born with special spiritual gifts."

"Do you think Mary Lee has special gifts? "

"Oh, Mary Lee — she's a lamb! " Jane felt a twinge of disappointment. "And she's lucky, I'd say; she's such a healthy girl in every way, as well as being pretty. And a good sport, isn't she, about working so hard? I never knew anybody so disorganized as her mother."

"But it's — it's kind of fun at the Stebbins house all the same."

"I know." Marion Greene's voice was a little wistful. "Pete and the twins like to go there; it must be relaxing in spite of all the muddle. Jane, do you think Pete and Mary Lee are becoming very much attracted to each other? "

" Yes, I do."

" Because, if so, it's the first time. Pete's always enjoyed being with girls in a casual sort of way, but he's never stuck with one for long or seemed to take it at all seriously. Of course, he'll be going east to school in September if he's well enough, and there's no reason to think he won't be. His father and I were hoping he'd want to stay here and have his senior year at Halford School, but I'm afraid he'd never consider it. There's the telephone, Jane; see who it is, will you? "

Jane went out to the hall and picked up the receiver. " Hello? "

" Is that you, Jane? Hi! " It was Pete's voice — and he sounded perfectly cheerful and ordinary!

" It was you I wanted to talk to," he went on. " No answer at the cottage, so I thought I'd probably find you at Greenlands."

" I'm — I'm terribly sorry you're sick, Pete."

" Considering that I brought it on myself and that you tried to stop me, it's nice of you to say you're sorry, whether you mean it or not."

" But I do mean it."

" I know you do. Why did you run away from the barbecue? Was it because I snarled at you? "

" Only — only partly."

" I wanted to say I was sorry about that."

" It's O.K. Pete — when you're back, you'll be a little more careful, won't you? "

" Most likely."

" And I'll go on with the car — the things I can do."

" Fine; you've learned a lot. I tell you what — you'd bet-

131

ter come in with Mother and Mary Lee this afternoon, and I'll explain what you can carry on with."

" Sure, Pete, I'll come; I'd like to."

" Be seeing you! "

As Pete hung up, Jane's father came in the front door.

" Oh — Dad! Aunt Marion's out in the kitchen, and I — I was just going to go back to the cottage to see if you were there and maybe wanted some lunch."

" Let's walk over together, then. I hoped you were here. I'll go in and give Marion a book she wanted, and ask after Pete."

As they set off along the footpath together, it seemed to Jane that her father was looking odd. Perhaps he didn't know how to start a conversation after having been so furious with her the night before.

" How did you know Pete was sick, Dad? "

" Your aunt saw me in Halford as she came back from Maryville this morning, and stopped and told me."

" Were you surprised? "

" A little — not very much, as a matter of fact. Marion's never said a word, but it's been clear enough that she's had something serious on her mind about Pete."

" I found out accidentally, Dad, but I've known all along."

" Poor chap — and poor Marion too; I hope it works out all right. There doesn't seem to be anyone without his share of problems. Jane, I didn't mean to be so brusque last night. I was worried, of course, thinking something had happened to you, but that wasn't any excuse to lose my temper. I know you're making serious efforts in a lot of directions this summer, and it isn't easy. I do appreciate it, Jane; your struggles with the cottage housekeeping, and in other things too."

" It's — it's perfectly all right, Daddy." Jane wished she

could say something more, but her father looked satisfied. It was wonderful when a grown-up person could admit being wrong. "Do you know what? Aunt Marion's going to help me pick out some clothes and fix my hair and things like that."

Dad looked a little sad. "If your mother were here — oh, that reminds me! I found a letter from Jean at the post office this morning. She says she's definitely coming back to America at the end of the summer, and wants to see us and talk over some 'ideas' she has."

"I think Jean's lonesome, Dad. That time she came to the cottage I told her I'd stay with her more this winter." Jane was impressed by the sound of her own voice — it was so firm and calm!

"Yes, I think you should." Dad smiled at her. "You're getting old enough to make a lot of your decisions — and I think this one's right. No one's going to keep you from maturing now! And something else I found at the post office, Jane, was a check. That article on Germany has been accepted and paid for, and the editor wants to see others. I'm beginning to see my way toward clearing some of our debts. Don't skimp on whatever clothes you need, pup. Figure out with Marion about how much it will take to outfit you and tell me. I know you've been spending your baby-sitting money on the cottage."

"Oh, Dad, that's nice about the article. And thank you for the clothes!" Jane wished she could say something more, to explain that she was proud of him about the article, but it had already been such an extremely personal conversation! Anyway, she would read it and try to understand it; maybe she could get hold of a copy to keep.

They had reached the picket fence around the cottage. Her father opened the little gate and walked through, but Jane hesitated a moment. Pete was sick; Pete cared very seriously for Mary Lee — so her heart was broken, wasn't it? But she didn't feel heartbroken; she felt a swell of hope and cheerfulness inside, and she vaulted over the low fence and ran to the door.

Chapter XIII

PETE's here! " Jane gave a start as her father's voice echoed up the cottage stairs. " He wants to know if you're ready."

" I'll be right down! " She went softly to her bedroom window and looked out. Pete was lolling on the grass under the apple tree, probably getting his good summer suit all stained. The sun made a dappled pattern through the leaves. How marvelous Pete's tan looked. That was because he went swimming almost every day now, usually with her and the twins.

She turned back to the bright, round mirror Aunt Marion had given her to replace the old mottled one that had distorted everything. She wasn't tan herself; Aunt Marion said she probably never would get really brown. But her skin had a faint color; that, and the rosy face powder, made the freckles less obvious! Her new blue-linen summer skirt and jacket looked nice. Would Pete notice what she was wearing? Would he like it?

She ran downstairs and out into the sun. " Here I am! "

" Good. Let's get started if we're going to walk. Mom's going to pick up Uncle Julian with the car later on. What about Kai? "

" He has to stay here. I didn't think the Bakers would want him at the wedding; he might come into the Meeting-house or knock over the cake or something. Do I — do I look O.K., Pete? "

"What? Oh, sure; you look fine! You've been looking more your age lately, haven't you? By the way," he added, as they turned from the cottage drive into the Halford Road, " I had a letter from Mary Lee. She says she's having a fine time at the lake and to say 'hi' to you in case she doesn't get around to writing. She's sorry she's going to miss the wedding. Let's see — I should have brought the letter, there was so much stuff in it to tell you. She says any time you can't stand it any more, taking over for her at her house, to let her know and she'll come back."

"Oh, I don't mind helping Gladys Stebbins. It's only that it keeps me awfully busy. Poor Dad has to get his own supper half the time or else eat at Eleanor's. What else does Mary Lee say?"

"Oh — big sensation at the lake. Nobody there could figure out what was wrong with Ed Marshall; he moped around, and then suddenly vanished without a word. Didn't anybody know he and Ginny Baker liked each other?"

"No. You know, yesterday I was helping Ginny decorate the Meetinghouse with flowers your mother brought over from Greenlands, and she started telling me about it. It all started before college closed, and they were practically engaged — and then they had a fight. Ginny says she can't even remember what it was about, and neither can Ed. So he went off to the lake, and she was miserable and he was miserable. Then they both wrote to say so — and their letters crossed each other! They decided they couldn't stand waiting till fall to get married, and besides, they wanted to go away for a honeymoon before Ed had to start working. I didn't think people who — who really love each other ever had fights."

"Oh, I don't know. Dull subject! Listen, Mary Lee took off in such a hurry I didn't quite get who it was that invited her to come. Was it one of the faculty families?"

135

"Yes, the Carmichaels. Larry Carmichael's at Halford School; he's a — a friend of Mary Lee's and his father teaches Latin. But Mary Lee will know everybody there."

"I hope she won't settle down there for the rest of the summer. How about this wedding, Jane — what's it going to be like? I never happened to go to a Quaker wedding before."

"I have; I've been to quite a few. Sometimes Halford students who are Friends get married in the Meetinghouse right after they graduate. It's a lot like Meeting for Worship. When it begins, everybody sits quietly, the way they do in Meeting. The people getting married sit up in front. After a while, when they feel like it, they get up and exchange vows. Other people speak sometimes — the way they do in Meeting, if they feel inspired. The vows are always just about the same. I mean, it's the man that begins, and he takes the bride's hand and says something like, 'I take thee to be my wife, promising through divine assistance to be unto thee a loving and faithful husband so long as we both shall live.' And she says the same thing, and that's all."

"That sounds all right. But wouldn't it be nice to dress it up a little with music or something?"

"Billy wanted to play his harmonica at the reception afterward."

"Billy's happy, isn't he?"

"Yes; I didn't think he would be."

"Why not?"

"Well, Johnny Baker, Billy's father, was awfully nice; he used to whistle when he worked in the drugstore, and take Billy fishing. Billy likes Ed, but you wouldn't think he'd want him to take his father's place."

"I don't think you're being fair, Jane. Even if Billy minded a lot, he's a sensible kid and old enough to realize that you couldn't expect Ginny to go on being lonesome all her life."

"She's got Billy."

"But he'll grow up and get married. And people *like* having husbands and wives. Anyway, Ginny would probably like to have some more kids. Then, what about the whole thing from Ed Marshall's point of view? You've always said he's such a good guy; it would be rough on him if he couldn't marry Ginny. Wilbur Baker's glad; he thinks it's fine; he told me so one time when he came to see me in the hospital."

"Oh, well, Wilbur doesn't mind things."

"I know. That's one thing about a lot of Quakers — the older they get, the better — like Roquefort cheese. I mean, they get to be sixty or seventy or eighty or ninety, but they don't sit around feeling sorry for themselves. They go right on trying to abolish capital punishment or stop wars or clean up slums. They don't seem to get discouraged. Did you know that Wilbur Baker's been going to Maryville twice a week for about fifty years? I must say, that old wreck of a car of his looks as if he'd run it about that long too. He's got one of the door handles tied on with rope."

"He does prison visiting, doesn't he?"

"Yes, in the county jail; and he goes to see people in the incurable ward at the hospital. They're all friends of his."

"You sound almost pro-Quaker, Pete."

"As a matter of fact — " Pete paused, picked a stalk of Queen Anne's lace, and put the stem between his teeth.

"As a matter of fact, *what?*"

"Wilbur Baker and I had some conversations while I was in the hospital, and he loaned me some books. Of course, I had time on my hands to think things over in general."

"Well, but what, Pete? What are you getting at?"

"I've still got to go into the subject a lot more, but I've decided there may be something solid in this Quaker business."

"I bet you're saying that now because you're not sick any more."

"That doesn't have anything to do with it."

"Well, what does, then?"

"Nothing new, exactly. It's hard to explain. I sort of saw it all differently — or felt different about it. I began by thinking about all the things that made me suspicious about religion. Diseases and wars and concentration camps and bombs and what not. Then I thought about how people have always tried to do something to help out — giving time and money and work, not because they get anything out of it. At least, nothing material. And how Quakers — I guess because we don't have any creed — don't turn up their noses at other religions. I talked with Wilbur Baker about that — other denominations, I mean. He said it's like people taking water from a river in different colored and shaped jugs and pitchers — but it's all the same water."

"But, Pete —"

"And, anyhow, how's a person going to live? I mean, just grabbing off as much dough as you can for yourself — or even for yourself and your family — is that any better than a pig stuffing himself if he gets a chance? What about the things that are good about people, and the things that are beautiful — art and flowers and mountains and music and so on? They're real, aren't they? Just as real as an atom bomb."

"But, Pete, you're making me feel all mixed up! This is totally different from what you've been saying all summer!"

" I was probably more or less arguing with myself all along. My mother and father may be pretty amazed if I give this Quaker thing a real whirl."

" I guess they'd be glad. I've talked about religion with your mother. She said the other day that she and your father will transfer their membership to Halford Meeting and be on committees."

" I guess they'd be glad, all right, but there are some problems coming up too. For one thing, we've got kind of a lot of dough — too much, probably; I know your dad thinks so — and I suspect we ought to give away a lot of it. I'll have to talk that over with them very seriously. And I don't know exactly what it's invested in, either."

" That's why Dad's never let Jean help us. I told you, her husband made most of his money out of something to do with the war and building airplanes."

" That's running it into the ground a little, not letting your grandmother help out when — " Pete paused.

" When we've had to borrow money, you mean, because of Mother being sick? "

" Wonders will never cease! " Pete said. " You used to be so sensitive about money, I wouldn't have dared mention the subject. I think Uncle Julian leans over backward on things like that, but I respect him for it."

" If you start criticizing your family, they'll most likely wish you'd stayed an atheist. And I feel very confused."

" You ought to make up your mind for yourself, Jane, and not let anyone influence you."

" Not anyone? Ever? "

" I don't know about that. One thing about you, you do keep your mind open. I mean, you're willing to change it if you're convinced. And I don't say you shouldn't listen to me; I've given all this stuff a lot of thought lately. Well, here's the Meetinghouse already! "

Jane, slipping into her old seat beside her father, and wishing that Aunt Marion and Pete weren't sitting so far behind them, wondered if she could concentrate on the wedding. There was so much to think over in what Pete had said on the way. But Ginny and Ed were walking slowly up the aisle to their seats facing the Meeting. How lovely Ginny looked in her gauzy blue dress, and as if she was frightened a little bit too! But Ed, his dark, ruddy face contrasting with his gray suit, was beaming. The Meetinghouse looked heavenly, with the sun pouring in! Was it because of the flowers — a big, brilliant vaseful on each window sill — or was it that this was the first time she had been in the building since the Sunday after Pete and Aunt Marion came to Halford? Daddy had said that the early Friends thought any kind of ornament was sinful, but that the Meetinghouses they built were accidentally beautiful anyway, because they had simple lines. The white walls looked clean and cool, and the fireplace had scarlet roses in it.

Dad's face looked quiet and rather sad; perhaps he was thinking about the time when he and Mother had been married here. Jean had told Jane that after the wedding she had gone away and cried because of Mother's not having been married in her own church.

Ginny and Ed were standing up now, and Ed was speaking, his voice very deep and startling and alive in the silence of the Meeting. Jane clenched her hands. It was foolish to cry at a wedding! But it was hard not to, now that Ginny was speaking, in her soft, pretty voice, almost stammering a little. The tears weren't real tears — or at least not sad ones. Was Pete having the same kind of reactions? Boys probably didn't.

Wilbur Baker was the first person to rise and speak in the silence that followed the vows. " I am moved on this occasion, Friends," he said, "to remember with joy the words of our founder, George Fox, that ' over the ocean of darkness and death there flows an ocean of love and light.' The Lord bless thee, Virginia, and thee, Edward, and may the light of his countenance shine upon you forever."

After that, nobody said anything at all, which was just as well, Jane thought, because nothing could have been as marvelous and impressive as what Wilbur Baker had said in his strong voice. Silence *was* different when it was a lot of people being quiet on purpose. It wasn't like the silence of an empty house or a field or the woods.

Everyone burst into conversation at the reception on the Meetinghouse lawn afterward. There were white linen cloths on the old trestle tables from the First Day School room, and they were flecked with leaf shadows, and even the cakes and some of the little sandwiches were decorated with flowers. Eleanor Digges was pouring fruit punch, and looking hot and excited.

Pete and Aunt Marion came over. "Wasn't it lovely!" said Aunt Marion. "Let's go through the receiving line together."

Wilbur Baker looked at Jane closely and patted her shoulder, and Ed's mother from Chicago shook hands, but Ginny kissed her and said, "Jane, thank you again, honey, for being such an angel to Billy all summer!"

Ed said: "How about your tennis, Jane? We'll settle down to some serious workouts after the honeymoon. Say, you're looking pretty cute today!" And he kissed her too, which was an odd feeling, because his cheek was not rough, exactly, but you could feel that Ed was very strong.

"Pete, doesn't the food look pretty? It's the way I imagine magic tables look — you know, when the hero arrives at the castle at night, and it's empty, but the tables cover themselves."

Pete laughed. " These didn't."

" I know. Ginny thought she'd have a caterer, because she wanted to ask everyone in Halford and some people from Maryville Meeting too, and there wasn't much time, but Eleanor wouldn't let her. Eleanor made most of the sandwiches, and I helped a little. Look, Pete, these little ones are lobster paste, and you like that."

" Jane! " Billy Baker bobbed up between them, looking very clean and unfamiliar in a stiff, new suit, his hair slicked down. His face was a little anxious. " Did you know Mom and Ed are going to Quebec? "

" Yes, but not for very long, Billy. After that, when they make trips, you'll go too."

" Harold Stebbins and I are going to sleep out in a pup tent in the Stebbinses' back yard. Mom said I could, and so did Harold's mother. Will you play tennis with me every day till Ed gets back? "

" Well, you have a nerve, Billy Baker! "

" Why have I got a nerve, Jane? "

" You put up with me when you don't have Ed — "

" But he plays a lot better than you because he's the coach, and anyhow — anyhow, he's my father now, I guess, isn't he? I mean, he practically is."

Billy's voice had a quaver in it, and Jane hugged him briefly, her slight feeling of resentment melting. It was silly to be even a little angry about something so minor.

" My father — my real father — " said Billy, " used to sing ' Casey Jones ' to me before I went to sleep. But I was a lot younger then."

" Billy, I'll play tennis with you every day I have time to. And some afternoon you and the Stebbins kids can come to Stepping Stones with me and the twins. Aunt Marion's having the old fireplace fixed, and we'll have a hot-dog roast."

"Great!" said Billy. "It's too bad Marion Greene can't go on living there instead of you and your pop, Jane. I mean, she and Pete's dad could probably do a lot of things. Make a ball field, maybe — or a private tennis court? How about that, Pete? Behind the barn would be a good place. There's Mom waving — I guess she wants me." He picked up a handful of the little sandwiches and ran off.

"What a brat!" said Pete, and laughed. "It was nice of you to say you'd play with him. I expect to be playing tennis any time now, myself. The doctor said I could by next week. So I'll take you on. I've seen you play, and you're pretty good for a girl. That's a mean-looking serve you have, but I'm warning you right now that I can beat you to ribbons. You won't like that."

"I guess I wouldn't actually care so much. I don't feel the way I used to about tennis. I always used to want to go on playing till it was so dark you could hardly see the ball."

Aunt Marion joined them. "Aren't the refreshments good — and wasn't it sweet of Eleanor to do them? Pete, your Uncle Julian wants me to read something he's working on, and we thought we might walk back, as it's such a nice day, and leave you to bring the car home."

"Sure — or maybe if Jane would like to, we'll take a drive somewhere first."

"Of course, dear. I must speak to Wilbur Baker. Here are the keys."

"How about it, Jane, since we've got the convertible? I want to talk to you anyway about what we were talking about on the way from the cottage. I had some more ideas during the wedding. Hey, I know what. We'll go have supper at the Tow Path Inn at Calmus — Mother and the kids and I went there with that friend of Mother's in Columbus. How far is it from here — about thirty miles?"

" It's about that. Pete, I'd love to. I haven't been there since I was a little kid and Mother and Dad took me. It's so nice! I remember we had one of the tables outdoors, and there were ducks swimming around on the canal. But I can't go."

" Of course you can. I'll go tell Mother and Uncle Julian, and we'll say good-by to Ed and Ginny and take off. You're all dressed for it too. I wouldn't take a girl in jeans to a nice place like that, let me tell you. All these little things to eat are making me hungry."

" But I have to go over to the Stebbinses' now."

" Oh, cut it out."

" I have to. I promised Mary Lee I'd help her mother two or three hours a day at least, or she couldn't have gone to the lake at all. I told Gladys Stebbins I'd come over now, so she can come to the reception with Arline and Harold and I'll stay with the little kids. There isn't anyone else to do it, because Mary Lee's father had to go to Columbus."

" Well — I'll wait fifteen minutes; she can come for that long while you watch the kids, and then we'll go."

" No. I have to stay and help her get supper. I said I would."

" It wouldn't make any difference for once."

" It would, Pete. It would make a lot of difference. It's a kind of matter of honor, almost. Just *because* I'm not getting paid, it's important to do what I promise. The kids like to have me come, and they're expecting me."

" I take it you don't want to come to Calmus very much."

" I do, though! You're being very unfair. You're pretending to think I don't want to go when you know I do. It's only because of having to do something else that I'm saying I can't."

" Don't be so righteous."

" What? "

" Oh — I mean, sort of holier-than-thou about this whole deal, as if you were a heroine or something. I bet you had some sort of reason — though I can't imagine what — for being so all-out helpful and sweet about volunteering to take over for Mary Lee. One thing about *her*, she doesn't make a big production over every little thing."

" I never heard anyone say anything so mean, Pete! "

What Pete had said was not only mean — it was untrue, besides! Why had she offered to help, so that Mary Lee could accept the Carmichaels' invitation? Had it been just in order to follow Aunt Marion's advice about doing things you ought to do — about being unselfish? Yes — so why did Pete's remark give her a sinking feeling? She looked at him despairingly. He was sulkily kicking his foot against a tree trunk; he was really cross with her.

But what Pete had said *was* true, too. She *had* had a special motive in offering to help Mary Lee, even if she hadn't completely admitted it to herself till now. In spite of the scene in the Meads' orchard, in spite of the amount of time Pete and Mary Lee spent together, Jane had gone on hoping. Had hoped, for instance, that if Mary Lee was out of the way for a couple of weeks —

" Make up your mind, Jane."

" I have. I absolutely can't go."

" All right."

" Too bad Mary Lee isn't here — you could take her! "

" Too bad is right. I'm going to take the car back — want me to drop you at the Stebbinses'? "

" No, thanks, I'll walk! "

" Suit yourself! " And he turned away.

" What's the matter, Jane? " Wilbur Baker was looking down at her. " Is thee leaving already? "

" I have to go to the Stebbinses', Wilbur Baker, so Mary Lee's mother can come to the reception."

"Thee's a good girl, Jane, to help Gladys Stebbins; she's never been much of a hand to manage."

"Wilbur Baker, suppose you do something that's right, only then you realize you did it for the wrong reason — or partly for a reason that *wasn't* a good reason — and you know you weren't telling yourself the truth about why you did something."

Wilbur Baker looked at her kindly. "Don't thee worry thy head about it, Jane. Thee's trying to find thy way honestly, and God will help thee if thee lets him. Take along some of the cookies and cakes for the little Stebbinses, and stop at the store on thy way and fill up a quart box of the special vanilla ice cream. Make sure thee eats a good plateful too — it will help fatten thee."

Talking with Wilbur Baker had helped, Jane decided, as she made her way to the Stebbinses' little house, the sounds of the reception fading behind her. But not much — and the convertible was gone. She went into the drugstore and began to fill a box with the rich, golden-white ice cream that Wilbur Baker always made himself. How lonesome the store seemed without a person in it, with only the loud, steady tick of the big wall clock to break the quiet! She and Pete hadn't had a real argument for ages — until now. It did sometimes seem as if the days that started out to be the best of all ended up being the worst.

She left the store and hurried to the Stebbins house so that the ice cream wouldn't start melting. A battered tricycle, lying on its side, blocked the door; she moved it away and went in.

"Hello, Jane!" Gladys Stebbins looked up with a smile. She was sitting at the kitchen table with a half-finished cup of coffee before her. "Don't you look sweet! Was the wedding nice?" Her pretty face, like a slightly worn and tired version of Mary Lee's, looked expectant, like a child's before a treat.

"It was lovely, Gladys Stebbins, and the reception started a little while ago, so you can go right on over. You look nice." It was true. Gladys Stebbins, who never, usually, managed to " catch up with herself," as she put it, had on a fresh, pretty dress.

" I even put my hair up in pin curls last night," she confided.

" Hi, Jane! " The children came rushing in from the yard as she put the ice cream in the refrigerator. " Jane's got refreshments from the wedding! "

Jane defended her parcel. " It's wonderful refreshments, only you and Arline can't have any, Harold, because you're going to the reception with your mother, so you'll have yours there. These are for the other kids."

" Oh, dear — that's right, of course; it wouldn't be fair." Gladys Stebbins looked flustered, and Jane realized that she would have shared the refreshments instantly among all the children.

" Yes, you'll have to wait, Arline and Harold," she now said, trying to sound firm. " But look at Arline, Jane! She's been ready for an hour, and I wanted her to stay in the house and keep tidy, but she insisted on playing in the yard. How can I take her looking like that? "

" She'll be all right." Jane pulled the little girl over to her. " I'll do over her braids, Gladys Stebbins, and go over her face with a washcloth; you brush Harold's hair, and they'll both look fine. When you're gone, the rest of us will go outdoors to eat and call it a picnic."

Gladys Stebbins hesitated in the doorway when the children were ready. " I won't stay long, Jane."

" You stay as long as it lasts, Gladys Stebbins, if you want to. I don't have anything special to do." Juney's grubby little hand clutched at her skirt, and she lifted the two-year-old child onto her lap. " Billy Baker will like having Harold there."

"Oh, Mom, come on!" Arline pulled at her mother's hand.

"Jane, what's that on Juney's face and dress? It looks as if she's gotten into something sticky!"

Five-year-old Stevie and his sister May, a year younger, looked at each other. "Juney was crying," Stevie volunteered, "so we gave her something to play with — out of a can, in the tool shed."

"I'll take care of it." Jane got Gladys Stebbins and the two children out of the house, feeling glad there was plenty to do. It would take her mind off the thought that she could now have been sitting beside Pete in the car on the way to Calmus.

"I know what, kids; let's get out the hose, and you put on bathing suits. You can all have showers out in the yard! That'll clean Juney off, and you'll all feel cooler, and then we'll have the picnic."

The children shouted at the prospect, and Jane, helping them change their clothes and hunt for the swimming suits, reflected that all the Stebbins children always seemed happy about almost anything. They hardly ever had any fights among themselves; their parents never seemed to find fault with them. They loved being in the same room together. During schooltime, when Mary Lee and Arline and Harold all did their homework in the living room with its overstuffed furniture, and with the television turned on, the little kids were always trying to dream up some reason to get out of bed and come downstairs and be in the living room too. Their mother and father let them stay "just a little while," till they fell asleep, finally, on the big, ugly sofa. Candy and Sandy liked coming to the Stebbins house — and so did Pete. How furious he had been with her at the reception! There wouldn't be any natural reason to see him tomorrow, because Aunt Marion was taking the twins to visit her friend in Columbus for the weekend. Perhaps Pete would go with them. When Mary Lee got back, he would probably take her to the Tow Path Inn.

"Come on, Jane!" May tugged at her. "We're ready. It will be a wonderful time!"

Chapter XIV

I THINK, Janey, thee could pack the berries a tiny bit tighter in the jars."

"All right, Eleanor; I'll be careful."

Eleanor's face was red from bending over the jam boiling on the stove. Her little blue-and-white kitchen, usually so tidy, was littered with peach skins and berry hulls. Jane saw with dismay that her own white blouse already had a long, purplish streak down the front.

"I know hardly anybody does preserving any more, but I love to see the jars on their shelf when it's done. We'll write labels out and glue them on later. And when this batch has boiled, we'll have a little snack together. It was a shame, Jane, to ask thee to help with the fruit when thee has so much to do at the cottage and at the Stebbinses' too. But I knew Marion Greene was going to Columbus today with the twins, so thee'd have more time than usual. Did Pete go with them?"

"I don't know, Eleanor."

"These peaches could have been put up two days ago, but I was so rushed with the wedding refreshments. Wasn't it a perfect day, and didn't dear Ginny look sweet!" Eleanor's eyes were a little moist. "The only prettier bride I've ever seen in Halford Meetinghouse was thy own mother, Jane. About the fruit — I thought maybe thee'd like to learn how to do it. Some of those old apple trees at Greenlands still bear, don't they? Applesauce is very easy to put up, and I could come and help thee."

"Goodness, Eleanor, I didn't mind coming today. Look how much you've been helping me at the cottage all summer!" Eleanor looked pleased, and Jane wondered why she had never said anything before about the help with the cottage renovations and housekeeping. "I wouldn't have time for a while to do any myself, but maybe if the apples are O.K. for sauce when we're back at Greenlands —"

"Thee still has thy heart set on that, Jane, dear, hasn't thee?"

"Of course. Daddy has too, if we can rent the cottage. Did you know Daddy sold another article, Eleanor?"

Eleanor nodded. "The last one I typed for him — the editor took it right away! I think it's wonderful! Doesn't thee feel thee's very lucky to have a brilliant father?"

Quick footsteps sounded on the garden path. Jane recognized them, and caught her breath as Pete came bursting in the kitchen door. He had stayed at Greenlands! But what was he doing here?

"Excuse my barging in, Eleanor Digges!"

"Why, Pete, I'm glad to see thee, dear!" Eleanor was flustered. "It's an awful sight in here, I know — My preserves —"

"Hi, Jane!"

"Hi." It was impossible not to respond to Pete when he smiled like that and, at the same time, looked at her rather cautiously. He was probably wondering if they were on speaking terms — and no wonder, after his unreasonable behavior yesterday.

"Listen, I've got an awful emergency coming up at Greenlands!" He flipped a kitchen chair around, and sat astride it with his elbows on its back. " I don't know what I'm going to do. I called the cottage, and Uncle Julian said Jane was here — "

" But what's the trouble, dear? "

" Mother took the car and the kids, you know, and went to Columbus; she's going to spend the day getting them clothes and stuff for school, and take them to a movie in the afternoon. I weaseled out of the deal, because I didn't want to hang around during the shopping. They're going to stay with that college friend of Mother's at some sort of cabin or old farm outside the city that she uses for a summer place, and it doesn't have a telephone. So I can't get hold of Mother, and right after she and the kids took off the Falcones called up and said they're driving through on the way to San Francisco, and would like to stop with us for a couple of days. I had to say yes. I mean, I wanted to, but it's an awful jam! How can I take care of house guests? There's somebody sick in Rachel's family, so she can't come — "

" Who are the people who are coming, Peter? "

" Oh — cronies of Mother's and Dad's. He's an Italian architect, but his wife's American, and they've got a boy, Mario. Jane knows about him; he's at school with me. He's one of my best friends. What am I going to do, Eleanor? I'll have to give them something to eat tonight — "

" Of course thee will."

" Mother left part of a cold ham, and I was going to make myself a sandwich for supper. But I don't even know where the sheets for the beds are! There's probably enough stuff in the house for breakfast, but I don't know exactly how much bacon or anything you need to feed three extra people. The Falcones have this fabulous apartment in Rome; we stayed with them for about a month once, when the twins were babies. And at home in New York they've got a whole slew of maids running around underfoot — "

" Now, Peter, don't thee go to pieces."

" But what am I going to do? I can get the next Maryville bus — "

Eleanor shook her head. " Thee wouldn't be back in time, using the bus, if thee wants to have a nice supper for thy friends. No, thee can take my car, Peter, if thee promises not to drive too fast, and go to Maryville. I'd go along myself, but the fruit's so ripe I don't dare let it wait. Take Janey with thee. Janey, thee have Alfred Hanson cut up a couple of nice broilers for thee, and thee can do them in the oven at Greenlands with jelly, the way I showed thee. Get some biscuit mix too, in case Marion doesn't have any on hand, and a head of lettuce. Wait, I'll make thee out a list. Save the cold ham for breakfast, Peter; thee can offer it in case thy friends would rather have it than bacon."

" Will you do it, Jane? " Pete looked at her hopefully.

" Of course she will! " said Eleanor. " I can finish up here perfectly well without her. And I'll make thee some of my tiny turnovers for dessert; the frozen ones are never quite as good."

" It's awfully nice of you, Eleanor — and you'll come over and eat with us, won't you? And you, Jane, naturally? "

" All right, but Dad will have to come too. If I'm going to cook, I won't have time to fix anything at the cottage."

" Sure, I want Uncle Julian. But won't it be a lot of people to cook for? I'll help — I'll do anything you tell me."

" I think I can do it. I'm better at organizing a meal now than I was that time you and your mother came to the cottage."

" Oh, Jane will manage nicely, and I'll help once I'm there, Peter. Roquefort dressing, does thee think, Jane? It's so easy. And see if Alfred has some endive."

" And fresh corn? "

" Yes. I'd count on two ears apiece — or perhaps three for the boys. And for tomorrow, beef, I think — then if thee wanted to have a picnic, Peter, thee could have it cold for sandwiches. Here."

" Oh, good." Pete took the car keys from Eleanor.

" I'll wash some of the stains off my hands, Pete," said Jane, " while you get the car out of the garage."

" O.K. I won't scrape the doors or run over the flower beds, Eleanor Digges — and thanks again! You're wonderful! "

" Janey, honey! " Eleanor waited till Pete was out the door before she went on. " I have a surprise for thee, but I must explain it. Thee sees, a couple of weeks ago, when I was looking in Meyers' department store for a wedding present for Ed and Ginny, I saw that they were having a big dry goods sale. As thee knows, I never can resist something like that, so I popped in and had a look around. And I saw a polished cotton I thought was so lovely I got three yards and a half and made thee a dress. I thought I'd give it to thee for thy birthday next week, but perhaps thee'd rather have it this evening." She hurried off and came back, holding the dress up for inspection. " I thought the pink would be becoming to thee, Jane, and I got a belt to match the tiny green leaves in the print. I made the skirt wide; that's the prettiest style for thee, since thy waist is so tiny. Marion Greene told me thy measurements; she said she's been helping thee plan clothes for school. Does thee like it, Jane? "

" I do like it, Eleanor — it's perfectly beautiful! It will be my first real party dress, and I'd love to have it for to-night. Isn't it lucky that I've got my new white sandals with heels that I wore for the wedding? "

" They'll be perfect with it. How I wish Jessica could see thee wear it! " Eleanor sighed as she began to wrap the dress in tissue. " We sometimes used to talk about the days when thee would be growing up Janey, and going to parties."

" Did you really? "

" Of course."

" But, Eleanor — Mother was so sensational-looking. And I'm always going to look more like Dad than I do like her."

" Thy father's a very scholarly-looking man! "

" I guess he is," Jane giggled. " Especially when I try to press his summer suits or trousers — I can't seem to get the hang of it — and he forgets to get a haircut."

" Thee has Julian's coloring, to be sure, and I'm so glad thee's letting thy hair grow and setting it. But thy features have more of a look of Jessica's than thee thinks, dear. What shall I wear tonight, Jane? Does thee think, perhaps, my blue dress with the square neck and the ruffle? "

" Let's see — " What real difference could it make what Eleanor wore? Her plumpish figure always looked very much the same, no matter what she had on. There was the car outside, with Pete looking impatiently out the window. " I know what — wear that white sunback you got when you visited your cousins, and your white linen pumps. And your lace stole, to dress it up, and your mother's amethyst pin."

" I shall, then." Eleanor looked happy.

" Hey! " Pete stuck his head in the door. " How about it? "

" Run along, dears."

" I'll drive carefully, Eleanor Digges; I swear it. No, I don't. Quakers can't swear because they always tell the truth anyhow — or so they claim. So I affirm it; I'll drive carefully. Have you got the list, Jane? Come on! "

Once on their way, Pete did not speak for a few minutes.

Then he looked at her sideways. " I didn't know if you'd be a sport and help me out, Jane."

" I was mad at you for being so mean at the reception, Pete. And — and I *was* right to go to the Stebbinses' when I promised."

" I know you were. Mary Lee's mother never gets to go anywhere. She told me today on the telephone she had a wonderful time. Say, did you know Mary Lee's home? "

" She is! Why, she was going to stay a week longer! "

" I thought so too. But after the Falcones called, I tried the Stebbins house before I called the cottage, and Gladys Stebbins said you weren't coming today."

" That's right, because her sister was coming over to visit and help with the children."

" Well, anyhow, she said Mary Lee got back this morning, by train, and she wasn't expecting her."

" If you don't have a car, it's the only way you can come from the lake; it's a poky kind of train that takes all night, and then you have to get a bus from Columbus to Maryville. But how peculiar — and didn't Mary Lee call you? "

" No. Her mother was worried — afraid something went wrong at the lake. She asked Mary Lee to come to the telephone and talk to me, but she wouldn't; she said she wanted to rest."

" Well, I'll call her first thing tomorrow," Jane said. Her heart had sunk at the news that Mary Lee was back, and she couldn't help feeling glad to think that at least she wouldn't be at Greenlands tonight. Yet Mary Lee *was* really her best friend of her own age — and it would be awful if she was unhappy or sick!

" It isn't like Mary Lee to be temperamental," said Pete, frowning a little. " Here — I guess we'd better concentrate on this. Is everything going to be all right, Jane? "

" Oh, sure it is. The shopping won't take long, and the

things I'm going to make are practically foolproof. There won't be much that has to be done at the house, because your mother always has everything just so. The beds in the spare rooms are probably all made up already."

"I never thought to look," Pete confessed meekly.

"Even if they aren't, I know where the nice sheets are, and it won't take more than a few minutes to get the beds made. We'll get some flowers to put in their rooms and in the living room; there's helenium in bloom right now in the garden, and plumbago."

"I thought that was a disease," said Pete. "Say, I was floored, having them come when Mother and Rachel were both gone. But it sounds as if you have everything under control. You're very efficient, Jane — and it *is* nice of you to help."

"I'd naturally want to do anything I could to — to give your mother's visitors a good time, after all she's done for me," Jane said.

She took out the grocery list and pretended to be scowling at it thoughtfully. But she felt as if her heart was bouncing up and down at the thought of the evening ahead. The pink-and-green dress *was* heavenly. Surely, surely Pete would look at her tonight, and really see her! And maybe like what he saw? She would never be even half as attractive as Mary Lee, but clothes and a little make-up and gaining weight *had* made a difference — as Aunt Marion had predicted. Everyone had noticed it — except Pete. Or, rather, Pete noticed, but only vaguely, and he still treated her in a brotherly, teasing kind of way, as if she was a lot younger than she was. Assuming that the wonderful, impossible thing happened and Pete got to like her in the way she cared about him — he would be going back east to school in a few weeks. Her heart sank at the thought. Or would that be less awful than having to watch him taking Mary Lee out in Halford?

"Hey!" Pete gave her a nudge. "I've said twice, we're here!" Jane saw, with a start, that the car was stopped outside Hanson's store. "If you have to daydream, why don't you pick a nice topic? You looked as if you were chewing on a slice of lemon!"

The kind, fat proprietor smiled at them as they came in. "Hello, Jane; hi, young fellow! My wife tells me it was a nice wedding — I couldn't leave the store to get to Halford for it."

"It was lovely, Alfred Hanson; I wish you could have come." Jane produced the shopping list.

"Something nice for your dad? I've got some pork in — a few chops? Or something cooler, a hot day like this?"

"No, we're shopping for Greenlands — for visitors." And Jane handed over the list. "Eleanor Digges said would you pick out the broilers yourself and cut them up? I'm helping and so's she, because my Aunt Marion is away."

"Company coming, eh? All right, don't worry!" He turned to call to one of his clerks, then paused and looked kindly at Jane. "Shopping for Greenlands!" he said. "That brings back the past, that does, and your mother driving in from Halford. Jessica Greene forgot her list as often as not — but it made the day for us all when she came in!"

Pete was looking anxiously at the meat counter. "It all looks so *uncooked*, Jane. Will it be all right?"

"Sure it will!" Her heart lifted suddenly. "It'll be better than that, and everything'll be fun!"

Chapter XV

"SAY, what kind of deal is this, anyhow?"

Jane looked up from the sink; Mario Falcone stood in the doorway, his dark eyes regarding her intently.

"The kitchen looks great," he continued, "so leave it be, girl, and come on into the living room."

Jane felt her cheeks getting hot. It was true that she was inventing jobs now. The sink certainly didn't need scouring, but she felt shy about joining the others. Was it because the Falcones were strangers — or did it have something to do with the way Mario had glanced at her now and then across the dinner table?

"What's going on in there, Mario?"

"Oh, a ball! Good old, hard-working Pete is changing records, but my mom and pop are dancing. They're very sentimental types and never miss a chance. And your pop is dancing with that lady in the white dress who keeps on talking all the time."

"My father's *dancing!*"

"Sure he is."

"I didn't even know he knew how!"

"Well," Mario admitted, "I've seen more flashy technique in my time, but there's a lot of life in that old boy yet. So come on." He looked approvingly at the pink dress as Jane took off her big apron. "I want to dance with you."

"But I don't know how, only square dancing. I've never tried regular dancing, except a couple of times with other girls."

"How come? Is it because this whole town is a Quaker place?"

"That's partly the reason."

"Never mind; you'll do fine, I bet. You look very well co-ordinated to me, Jane."

"Hi!" The screen door banged as Billy Baker burst in before they could leave the kitchen. "I wanted to see you, Jane. Eleanor Digges was in the drugstore tonight buying some perfume, and she said she gave you a new dress today ahead of your birthday because there was a party. So I thought I'd bring over my birthday present for you to wear with the dress. I biked to Maryville for it so as not to have to pay the bus fare too. It's only from the five-and-ten," he added, suddenly looking doubtful as he dug a small package from his jeans pocket. "Maybe you won't like it. But it cost more than a dime, Jane, and I paid for it out of my own money."

The present was a rhinestone pin, an elaborately curved and flourished letter *J*. Jane fastened it carefully on her dress, feeling close to tears. "I do like it, Billy. I love it. It was sweet of you to bring it all the way out here so I could wear it tonight! This is Mario Falcone, Billy, Pete's friend from New York."

"Jane doesn't usually talk like that!" said Billy, looking at them both suspiciously. "I figured I might as well bring the pin out — and I thought maybe there'd be something interesting to eat around."

"I know, Billy; I'll put some of Eleanor's little turnovers into a bag. You take them home for you and your grandfather. I suppose, with your mother away, you and Wilbur Baker are living on hamburgers and frankfurters."

"We'll come over to the cottage for supper sometime soon," Billy offered. Taking the bag Jane gave him, he headed for the door so quickly that she had barely time to run after him and kiss him.

"Hey!" He stopped, glared, and rubbed his forehead where the kiss had landed. "I thought you were one girl that didn't go for all that stuff, Jane! You used to be a lot more like a boy! I was going to get you a horn for your bicycle, but I asked Marion Greene and she said she thought you'd *like* something to wear." Shaking his head gloomily, he went out the kitchen door and vanished in the soft summer night.

Mario was laughing. "I don't think you're much like a boy at all. And do you go 'for that stuff'?"

"Oh, Billy was just talking." Jane felt herself blushing again.

"Let's go and dance anyway." He took her hand and ran with her to the living room, where music poured from the record player. There Eleanor, looking quite nice in the white dress that wasn't as fussy and frilly as the clothes she usually wore, was dancing with Dad, as Mario had said, and they both looked very cheerful. Mario's handsome parents paused to greet them as they came in.

"Sensible boy!" said his father. "I was about to go and fetch our pretty little cook myself."

"But Eleanor planned the dinner — I mean, there was nothing to it — anybody could fix the chicken that way —" How idiotic to start jabbering about the chicken!

"It was sensational." Mario put his arm around her waist. "Now relax and follow me."

"Is — is this all there is to ballroom dancing?" Jane asked presently. It felt marvelous when the wide pink skirt swirled around her as they moved to the rhythm of the music.

"Absolutely all. You were kidding, weren't you, when

160

you said you didn't know how? "

" I wasn't — honestly. I didn't think I could do it. It's — it's easier than tennis."

" And so different! " Mario gathered her in a bit closer to him.

" Do people — I mean, is this how close people always dance together? "

" I don't know about *people*. But if you mind, tell me. I probably won't pay any attention."

When the record ended, Mario, without taking his arm from her waist, looked around him at the living room. It was even more beautiful than usual tonight, softly bright with flowers and lighted chiefly by the candles she and Pete had put in the fragile, old pink-and-gold porcelain candelabra.

" What a house! " Mario said. " It's the kind of place my pop's mad about. He's doing a book with lots of pictures about old American houses; that's one reason we're driving on this trip, so he can stop and do drawings and take pictures. Maybe he'd like to stick around here a few days and put this house in the book, if Pete's mother didn't mind having it in."

" It's our house, Mario. My father and I live here usually, but we're renting it for the summer. So I guess my father would be the one to ask about the pictures, but I'm sure he wouldn't mind. It's been in magazines a couple of times before, especially this room." Jane realized with surprise that she hadn't felt the least bit bothered by Mario's assumption that Greenlands belonged to the New York Greenes. He had probably taken it for granted that it was the official president's house.

" Oh, is it your place? Then Pete's father won't get to live in it, will he? He and my old man are a lot alike that way — I mean, getting a big bang out of old houses."

" What's Uncle Charles like, Mario? I've never met him."

"He's a lot like Pete, or vice versa."

"In what way?"

"I never thought about it much, but they've both got lots of personality. They're the sort of guys you notice, if they're in the room. And another thing, now that I think about it — they're both used to getting their own way."

Pete put on another record and walked over to them. "Hey, Jane! I thought Mary Lee said you didn't know how to dance."

"I don't know how. Mario's teaching me."

"Good for him."

"Hey!" Mario grinned. "Why don't you pat us both on the head? Who do you think you are — our aged uncle or something? Come on, Jane; let's try this one, it's faster."

"I'll dance it with Jane myself. How about it, Jane?" Pete stepped forward, slightly in front of Mario.

"Was there any iced coffee from dinner, Jane?" Dad had come over to them. "Eleanor would like some, and perhaps the Falcones would too."

"I — I think so. I'll be right back!" Jane hurried to the kitchen, glad to have a chance to catch her breath. Dancing with Mario and the kinds of things he said had made her feel rather flustered. Now there was the prospect of dancing with Pete — real dancing, held in his arms! Would she be able to follow him? Or would she fall all over his feet?

There were footsteps outside — who could it be? Had Billy come back for something? But the kitchen door opened, and there was Mary Lee, looking wonderful, Jane noted despairingly, in a scarlet cotton strapless dress.

"Hi, Jane!"

"Hi, Mary Lee. I — I heard you were back from the lake. Your mother told Pete. I thought you were going to stay at the Carmichaels' another week."

"Well, I intended to." Mary Lee sat down at the kitchen table. "The trouble was, I had a fight with Larry. It was about Pete, and we both got pretty sore. I rushed back to the cottage and talked Larry's mother into driving me to the train at Montgomery while Larry was still down by the dock. She didn't want to, but I cried and made a fuss. I wasn't sure I'd want to go anywhere today. But Mom said when Pete telephoned he said some people from New York were coming" — she hesitated — "and for me to come on over tonight if I felt like it."

"Yes, they're here, Mary Lee. It's that boy Pete talks about, Mario, and his parents. I'm sorry about the fight with Larry, but it — it's nice you could get here tonight."

"How's Pete been? He wrote that he was fine."

"Oh, he is! Perfectly O.K., the doctor says."

"Wonderful! I suppose that means he'll definitely go back east to school, though. Let's go in the living room — Hey! "

"What? "

"I like that dress — and your hair fixed that way, Jane! I never saw you looking so nice before."

"Eleanor made me the dress and gave it to me in advance of my birthday. I — I'm glad you like it. Look, you go on in; I'm going to fix up an iced-coffee tray."

When Jane got back to the living room, Mary Lee was already dancing with Pete.

"There you are! " Mario took the tray from her hands. "Who's the girl? " he asked. "I mean, we were all introduced, but who is she? Girl friend? "

"Mary Lee? She's a friend of mine, and — and a pretty close friend of Pete's. She's been away; she just got back to Halford today. She's very popular."

"Is she? That's nice."

"Don't you think she's pretty? "

" Sure! But I like little girls, with light hair. What's Pete been griping about? He wrote me once that nothing ever happened around here and that there was hardly anyone around under about sixty except a lot of little kids. Aha — here's a waltz. Good! On these I really let myself go."

Mario seemed to take it for granted that he and Jane would dance together, even though Mary Lee was looking over at them expectantly and even steering Pete in their direction. But perhaps Mario was only being polite. He had admitted he thought Mary Lee was pretty; of course he wanted to dance with her! The thing to do would be to give him a chance to get rid of her gracefully. Pete, of course, would most likely stand around and wait his chance to dance with Mary Lee again. The record ended. " I'm kind of out of breath, Mario."

" You don't sound it. What's going on? Didn't you like the waltz? "

" Yes — but maybe I'd better sit down for a while and rest."

" Whatever you say. We'll go out on the terrace and cool off; how about it? "

Even though Mary Lee and Pete started in their direction again, Mario calmly led her out onto the terrace, closed the French doors behind them, and when she sat down on the long wicker chair, perched on the low balustrade close to her. " It smells wonderful out here! " he said.

" That's because this is where the garden starts. It's too dark to see it. If you and your mother and father stay awhile, you'll be here when Aunt Marion gets back."

" I like Mrs. Greene. Once when I was a kid she helped me out of a stupid jam I'd gotten myself into. It was something very personal, and for some reason I couldn't stand the idea of telling my own mother or father about it. I don't know why, because I get along with them fine, usually. But seeing Mrs. Greene wouldn't be the reason I'd be glad if we stick around for a while."

"Pete told me a lot about you and the other people he knows at school."

"Yes, old Pete's quite a wheel at school. It was rough on him, getting sick last spring. But he looks healthy as a horse now. What could we do tomorrow, Jane? Go for a hike? Is there any place to swim?"

"Yes — there's a place I could show you, if you wanted to go."

"And I can get the car at night; Dad's pretty reasonable about it."

"Then — then maybe we could go to the movies at Maryville. I mean, if you had the car and if it seemed like a good picture — and if you felt like it."

"Why not? I'll tell you one thing you can't do around here that's really the greatest, and that's sailing. Did Pete ever tell you about the *Bonnie Belle,* my boat? We race her sometimes; she's a Lightning, a real beauty. I keep her out on Long Island; my folks have a kind of shack there for summers. Next time you come east, you'll come and stay, won't you? I'll take you out in her and teach you to sail; you'd take to it naturally."

"I've never been in the East at all."

"Haven't you? Well, it's about time you came. I could show you around. Maybe you'd like to come to one of the dances at school sometime? Hey — who's that on the bike?"

"Why — for goodness' sake!" Jane stared in surprise as a tall rider braked, came to a stop, let his bicycle fall on the path that ran past the terrace, and came slowly toward them. "It's Larry Carmichael — but how come he's here? There isn't any train from the lake again till tomorrow."

" Jane, is that you? " Larry came to the terrace.

" Hi, Larry! Sure it's me. How did you get to Halford? I thought — "

" Well, that's all right, then! " said Larry, interrupting her. " You shook me up for a minute. I thought for a minute, Jane, that you were your mother! You know, when she and your dad used to sit out here summers." He turned and glared at Mario. " Is this — ? "

" This is Mario Falcone, Larry — and that's Larry Carmichael." She couldn't think of any way to explain Larry's presence to Mario. " His father teaches Latin at the college."

Larry's face had cleared; the boys shook hands and Larry peered into the living room. " I don't see Mary Lee. Isn't she here, Jane? "

" Yes, but she didn't say you were coming home, Larry. She said — " Jane stopped.

" I don't care what the girl said. It's what she did — and I'm here to tell her exactly what I think about it."

He pushed open the French doors, said, " Aha! " and as Pete danced past with Mary Lee, Larry swiftly reached in and pulled her out onto the terrace.

" Hey! " Pete followed and stared at Larry in astonishment.

" Larry! " Mary Lee looked dumfounded too. " What are you doing here? "

" That's exactly what I came to ask you! " Larry said. " Of all the sneaky tricks! Mom said you threw a fit of hysterics and made her take you to the train. And who's this? *Pete*, I take it! "

" I never heard of such a thing! " Mary Lee's voice was shaking with rage. Mario got up and quietly closed the French doors. " Coming here and making a fuss in — in public! Well, I don't have anything more to say than I told you down on the dock. I never want to speak to you again."

166

" And this," Mario murmured in Jane's ear, " is the place where nothing ever happens? "

" Now, look, Mary Lee, I know I probably said a couple of things I shouldn't have — I was sore, and I was trying to make you sore too — but you should have known I didn't mean them. I was sick of hearing you talk about Pete Greene."

" What goes on? Who is this guy? " Pete demanded.

" It — it's Larry Carmichael from the lake." Mary Lee suddenly sounded subdued and hesitant.

" Are you his property, or what? "

" No, I'm not." Mary Lee's voice was faintly defiant. " We used to go around together once in a while — "

" Once in a while? " Larry repeated. " Once in a while, Mary Lee? " He sounded hurt, and not angry any more. " Look — I guess I didn't get it, and we are through this time. I didn't know you meant it. But you shouldn't say, ' Once in a while.' You went around with other guys now and then, but ever since we were in the first grade — "

" Larry! " Mary Lee interrupted him, her voice sharp. " Why are you holding your arm that funny way? "

" I smashed up the car," Larry muttered.

" *You did what?* "

" I took the car without asking Dad, because I knew he wouldn't let me have it to come all the way here. I drove too fast, and I ran it into a tree outside of Columbus. So I left it in a garage there and called Dad to tell him, and hitched to Maryville. Then I missed the last bus and had to walk to Halford. Your mom said you were here, so I borrowed Harold's bike and came out. I don't know what's the matter with my arm — didn't stop to find out. Banged my head against the windshield too, when I crashed." He rubbed his forehead. " But there wasn't any way to get here today except by driving."

" Well, of all the dumb things! " Mary Lee took a step

167

toward Larry, who sat down suddenly on one of the terrace chairs. " Pete — go ask Mario's father if you can have his car to take Larry in to Maryville to the doctor. You'll have to stay at our house tonight, Larry, so Mother and I can take care of you. You've probably got a concussion or something. Go on, Pete — what are you waiting for? "

" Well, but, Mary Lee! " Pete was almost sputtering.

" Hurry up. This could be very serious."

" It doesn't matter," said Larry sulkily. " I'll get Wilbur Baker to look at my arm tomorrow. And I can get into our house by the cellar way and sleep there."

" Try not to be utterly ridiculous! " said Mary Lee.

" Well, what's the big idea? " Larry asked. " What's the point of making a fuss about my arm if you don't — ? "

" If I don't what? " Mary Lee took another step toward Larry. " Oh," she said, " of all the fool things to do! " But her voice was very soft. " Your dad must be wild — and I don't blame him. Oh — of all the fool, fool things to do! You — you complete idiot! " And she sank down on the marble terrace paving and put her head against Larry's knee. He looked down at her, and after a moment or so put his hand gently on her head.

It wasn't right, Jane realized, for anyone else to be on the terrace. This was a very private moment for Larry and Mary Lee. She turned to go back into the living room just as Mario stood up, put one hand on her arm, and with the other nudged Pete, who was looking completely dazed. Then, as Pete did not move, but kept on staring at Mary Lee, who had now closed her eyes, Mario said, " What do you expect from a girl, anyway — consistency? " When Pete still did not move or speak, he gave him a little shove and said: " Hey! Wake up, move along, the doctor — remember? Let's go promote the car. What's the matter with you, anyway, dear boy? Don't you know when you're not wanted? "

168

Chapter XVI

"Do you hear something, Jane?" Mario was prowling restlessly around the cottage kitchen.

"Hear something! I certainly do!"

The sound of the car horn became more insistent.

"My parents seem to think it's time we shoved off. They said they'd pick me up at the foot of your driveway."

"I didn't think you'd be over again before you all left," Jane said. If she *had* thought so, Jane reflected, she wouldn't have let herself be found washing the cottage kitchen floor, surrounded by rags, mops, and buckets, and with her hair tied up in a kerchief!

"You look cute!" Mario said. "It's been a lot of fun. I wish we didn't have to go for a while yet. Look, Jane — I'll write to you from San Francisco." Another honk sounded. "I guess we're on our way." He looked younger somehow this morning, Jane thought, and he wasn't acting as poised as usual. It *had* been fun, wonderful fun, having Mario find her attractive — no wonder girls enjoyed it! "Jane, good-by!" said Mario suddenly and loudly. He pulled her to him, kissed her, and rushed down the little hall and out the front door.

"A fine sight, I must say," remarked a leisurely voice.

Jane spun around at Pete, who pulled open the screen door and sauntered in.

"There's no point in glaring at me," he said.

"Why didn't you say you were there? That's — that's spying! "

"Oh, cut it out. I didn't have any idea that Mario would talk his folks into stopping by here before they left. I came over to bring you a couple of presents. Mom says it's your birthday."

"Presents! You can't use presents as an excuse to — "

"To what? Look, I only happened to appear in time for the big romantic moment. I didn't have time to go away or yell or whatever you seem to think I should have done. Anyway, I didn't think you'd behave like that."

"*Like what?*"

"Oh, never mind, cool down. Look." He offered a couple of packages. "This little one is from Mom; it's a garnet bracelet that used to belong to my grandmother — Dad's mother, so it's a Greene family thing. And mine's a book, a manual on car repairs. I thought with Mario gone, you'd have time to work on the car again — for a change. You'll understand what you're doing much better if you read it carefully."

"First kindly explain what you meant, Pete, by saying you didn't think I'd behave ' like that.' "

"Oh — you know what I mean. Kissing a boy, by daylight — "

"What's daylight got to do with it? How come you feel entitled to criticize me? I suppose you're going to claim you never kissed anybody? "

"Sure I have! " Pete looked startled. "But that's different."

"It is? "

"Of course it is. Why, you don't really know Mario, for one thing — even though he has been hanging around here twenty-four hours a day for several days."

"You must be out of your mind, Pete, if you think I'll

stand for you talking like that. You let me decide for myself how well I know Mario — or anybody else."

"Incidentally, was that the first time he kissed you? After all, he's my friend. That's what you don't seem to be realizing, Jane — that I feel kind of responsible. I'm your relative, and older — "

"Pete!"

"O.K., O.K.! I'll shut up. I suppose you figure it's your business — "

"Will you please stop harping on it!"

"All right, let's drop the subject. Now, can you come over and work on the car? I think it's coming along."

Jane shook her head.

"Oh, come on. Do you like the bracelet?" he asked, as Jane took it from its tiny box.

"It's lovely." Jane slipped on the double row of dark-red stones in their quaint gold setting. "It's the first jewelry I ever had — except Billy's pin — and it's typical of your mother to think of something perfect to give me."

"I'll tell her you like it. Or you can tell her yourself, if you'll come on over, instead of stalling because you're mad at me."

"It isn't that. And thank you for the book, Pete — it was nice of you to give me a present. I'll read it carefully. I *am* still a little mad at you, but I'll get over it. The reason I can't work on the car is because I'm going to paint the hall this morning. It won't be long before we'll be trying to rent the cottage to someone. You know, for money to help run Greenlands — "

"Oh, Greenlands!" Pete sat down on the window seat and put his arms around his knees. "You *are* stubborn, aren't you? Once you get an idea in your head, no matter how silly — "

"What's silly?"

"This whole Greenlands deal. Nobody but you thinks it makes any sense for a minute."

"Nobody except my father, for instance! He wants to go back to our own house as much as I do."

Pete shook his head. "He hasn't told you, but he's changed his mind. He'd like to sell Greenlands. Eleanor doesn't want it —"

"Eleanor!" Jane's hands tightened on the car-repair manual. "What are you talking about? What's Eleanor got to do with it?"

"That does it!" said Pete. "That tears it! If I could only learn to keep my big mouth shut —"

"Go on; explain."

"Uncle Julian was going to tell you today, as a matter of fact, if he could get up the nerve, so I might as well. The thing is, he's gotten over the way he felt at first when we moved in. He's been saying he doesn't want to try to keep the place up, out of his income, and pay taxes on all the land, and so on. For one thing, it wouldn't be fair to the house; it would get run down. He'd like the trustees to buy it if they still want it for the college. And as for Eleanor —" He looked at Jane cautiously and stopped.

"What about Eleanor?" Jane felt that she knew.

"It was Eleanor who finally helped him decide, Jane. She thinks the same thing — that Greenlands ought to be the president's house and belong to Halford College. And — well, they're engaged, Jane. I think they settled it the other night, the day the Falcones came. They'd like to get married this fall sometime. Hey!" He slipped down from the window sill and walked toward her. "You're looking very peculiar, Jane. Are you going to faint or something?"

"No. Because I don't believe it. Eleanor must be making it up. My father wouldn't do that. He wouldn't marry

172

Eleanor; he wouldn't marry anyone in the world after being married to my mother."

"You're shaking!" said Pete. He pushed her down into the rocker beside the fireplace, and, sitting down beside her, looked at her intently. "Boy, you're taking this hard. Jane — do you realize you've got a kind of thing about your mother?"

"What!"

"Look, don't get excited before I even start. But you know — all this about Aunt Jessica — "

"All what?"

"I mean, all this that you've built up. She was O.K. — "

"Pete!"

"I don't mean that or not the way it sounded. You're getting me rattled! Everyone knows she was terrific-looking and had all kinds of personality and was fun to have around — and she was a good artist too. Naturally people were bowled over. But, Jane — you've built it all up to the point where a person listening to you would think she was too wonderful to be human. I don't know much about it, but I've heard my mother and father talking, and I've pieced things together. One reason Uncle Julian's so hard up now is because your mother did run through a lot of dough. I guess she was used to having it before she got married."

"She — she was sick for a long time." Jane leaned her head dizzily against the back of the rocker. She ought to tell Pete to go away, but something kept her in the chair. She clutched the arms; her palms felt wet and cold. She had to hear what else Pete would say.

"I mean before she was sick. Her paintings began to sell just about then, didn't they? She never wanted to bother with running a house; that's why there was always such a slew of people working at Greenlands. Having the garden made bigger, and going abroad, cost a lot. I mean — the whole thing wasn't much help to your father in doing *his* job."

" I don't want to hear anything else! "

" I'm sorry. That's all I was going to say, anyhow, and it's nothing so terrible. I wouldn't have brought it up at all if you didn't have this idea about your mother being so completely perfect that it would be an — an insult to her memory or something if Uncle Julian got married again. That's ridiculous, and it isn't fair to Eleanor."

" If it's true that they're engaged — "

" Jane — wait! " Pete interrupted her. " Please don't say anything rash! Look, I'm probably making a mess of this whole business, but as long as I've started I'll go on. Mom gave me a long letter to read, a couple of weeks ago, that she was sending to Dad. Most of it was about what the doctor said about me and going back to school and so on. She forgot that there was quite a lot of stuff in it about you too, that psychological double talk she goes in for, but I think I got what it all boiled down to. You loved your mother, sure, and you wanted to think she was perfect — because that would mean that somebody who was as wonderful as that loved you. Only — now, listen, because this part sounds screwy — at the same time you were jealous of her, just a little bit and 'way underneath somewhere. Because she was so sensational and because she was the one your pop always thought about first. A lot of girls feel like that, Mom said in the letter, but they won't admit it to themselves, and they get tangled up. You wouldn't call yourself Jessica, for instance, because you wanted to be completely different from her. And you've suspected these underneath feelings, so that's been giving you a guilty — "

" *Pete, stop talking about it!* "

174

" O.K., O.K.! Probably Mom should have been the one to talk to you if anybody did. Now you are sore at me, and you don't believe a word of it. I thought I ought to see if I couldn't talk you into a little bit of sense about this Eleanor business, since I did let it slip out."

" And — and that's why Eleanor's been making up to me — ? "

" Oh, cut it out! Hasn't she been nice to you all your life? She was crazy about your mother, and she's always wanted to do things for you because you're Aunt Jessica's child. But she's been in love with your father all her life. Mom and I could both spot that before we'd been in Halford a week."

" So it's been a regular campaign! Typing his articles, asking us to meals — doing all kinds of things for me so Dad would think how wonderful she was. And — and you and Aunt Marion saw what was going on, and pretended to be my friends, and didn't warn me — Oh, it's so sneaky! "

" Warn you? Warn you about what? That's where you're 'way off — this isn't a — a disaster! I've told you before — you scare Eleanor, so she sounds a lot dumber than she is. She's really nice, and I think the whole thing's great. Uncle Julian's kind of a clammed-up guy, and it's hard for him to admit he likes anybody — or to think that somebody could like him. Now he'll have a person who thinks he's wonderful revolving around him and taking care of him and fussing about him. Most girls get jumpy at the idea of having a stepmother, I guess, but this is different. Uncle Julian isn't ringing in someone on you that you don't know, and Eleanor will love mothering you if you'll let her. Here's Uncle Julian now! "

Dad's coming into the kitchen made it all real; there was no point in asking whether it was true. It *was* true; nobody had made it up. He and Eleanor would be married this fall, and they would sell Greenlands. She got up, her face averted in order not to look at her father, and started for the door, but Pete grabbed her arm.

" Jane — Pete — what's the matter? What's happened? "

" Jane's gone into a tail spin, Uncle Julian. I'm sorry — I let something slip out about selling Greenlands — and about you and Eleanor."

Jane looked at her father. " Pete's told me everything. And — and now I realize what's been going on all summer. I can't stop you from getting married, Dad, I know that — and you never do anything I want to, anyhow — but I'm not going to live in the same house with you and Eleanor. And I'll never speak to her again."

A quick yank freed her arm from Pete's hold, and she ran out the back door. Kai, roused from his nap in a patch of sun, jumped up to run by her side. Jane glanced swiftly over her shoulder when she reached the Stepping Stones path; there was no one following, but she continued to run and run, faster and faster, until the glimmer of the pond showed she had arrived. She did not know if the sounds she was making came from running — or was she crying? Anyway, it hurt, and it was hard to get her breath, but she was safe. They would leave her alone, thinking she would " get over it." She had got away; she could drop down flat in the warm grass and lie perfectly still and try not to think about anything at all, one arm around Kai's warm, strong, furry body.

Jane sat up with a jerk and opened her eyes. She felt stiff and rather hungry. How queer — she must have fallen asleep, and slept for a long time too, for the gold rays of the sun were slanting through the white birches from the west. She had got up feeling tired that morning, she remembered, because of being up late every night during the four days of Mario's stay — those four lighthearted days that seem so far away now. Yet they had ended only this morning when Mario went away. And then Pete came and told her all those things she didn't want to start thinking about yet. Kai was sitting beside her, his ears pricked up.

"Jane!" Her father's thin figure came into view on the path. "Jane!" he called again, urgently, "don't go rushing off! We must talk, and I promise you I haven't come to try to persuade you into anything you don't want."

"All right." How mournful his voice sounded! He came slowly along the edge of the pond and sat down on the grass beside her. His face was pale and unhappy. Well, she might as well talk with him now as later about — about everything. They would have to discuss how she could go away. Certainly she didn't intend to stay in Halford. Greenlands would be sold, and Dad was going to — to replace Mother with Eleanor, and Pete would be away at school. Pete didn't care about her anyway, even now that he didn't have Mary Lee, who had gone back to the lake with Larry. Perhaps she could still go and live with Jean. Or go away to boarding school.

"Jane." Dad touched her hand hesitantly. "You must believe me when I tell you I had no idea you'd be so terribly surprised and upset by this news about Eleanor. I knew you'd mind about the house, but as to Eleanor — well, she's always been like a member of the family! She's so fond of you, and I thought you'd been getting along so much better with her, and with me, and with people in general this summer. I know you like Marion, and I figured it was partly her influence."

"I thought Aunt Marion was my friend, and she pretended she was. All the time she was egging you on to marry Eleanor and not warning me —"

"Oh, Jane!"

" Yes, and plotting to keep Greenlands for herself! "

" That's morbid. It simply isn't true. Marion thinks the marriage would be a good idea, but her first concern when I told her was for you. She wondered how you'd take it, but we both hoped it would be all right. In fact, we thought that perhaps you suspected it."

" I never suspected it."

" Marion *is* your friend. She admires you. She thinks you have tremendous qualities of perseverance and affection and loyalty. She feels, as I do, that you've made a wonderful start this summer on overcoming some of your problems. I know it's been a hard pull, Jane, and I haven't known how to be as helpful as I would have liked to be."

" Well — " Jane began, and stopped. It wasn't much use talking about anything that *had* happened. The point was, what was going to happen now?

" I thought you were here," her father went on slowly. " I knew Kai was with you, so I didn't worry. I hoped you would come back to the cottage, and it took me awhile to decide to come after you, because I had to make a clear decision first. I've done it now. I won't go against your wishes in this matter of Eleanor."

Jane had not been looking at her father; now she turned her head, startled, and stared at him. " You mean — ? "

" I mean I'll give up the idea." He tried to smile. " It will be a ' consensus decision ' between us. You know — like the way we settle things in Friends Meeting for Business, where we never transact anything if there's even one person in the Meeting who objects to it. That's because Friends don't think it's right to override a minority. And you're not a minority, pup! You're half the family. So I'll tell Eleanor tonight. What's more, I promise you I won't act like a martyr about it."

" Oh, Dad, I wish I *could* feel differently."

"As to Greenlands — I haven't made any decision yet. I wouldn't have made any final one without consulting you, of course, anyway. I called the bank in Maryville after you went rushing off here, and had another talk with the manager. It isn't going to be easy, and we'll have to let some debts hang over us for a while that I'd hoped to start paying off, but with a bank loan we can swing it for a year at least, and then we'll have to see. In other words, you can count on being back in your own room a few weeks from now. How's that? Does that make you feel better?"

"Oh, it does! Of course it does! Why wouldn't it make me feel fine, having things the way I want them!"

"That's all settled, then. How about coming back to the cottage now? You must be starving."

Jane realized she didn't want to leave Stepping Stones right away. "May I stay here a while? I'm not very hungry. Maybe a few minutes, and then I'll come back to the cottage."

"All right, pup." He unfolded his long legs, stood up, then suddenly put his hand in his pocket. "Before I forget, I've got a birthday present for you, Jane."

"Oh, Dad — you gave me that dresser set this morning at breakfast!"

"Well, that was mostly Eleanor's idea. She helped me pick it out. This is something I thought of myself, this afternoon." He pulled out a little morocco case, its gilt and scarlet faded with age, and opened it. "Look, it's the little string of pearls that were thy great-grandmother's, Jane, and I gave thy mother this seed-pearl locket with the diamond *J* on it the day we were married. She always wore the pearls and the locket together — and I'd like thee to have them now."

"I'd love to, Dad. It's a beautiful present. Thank thee." It seemed strange to be using plain speech with Dad —

179

the last time he had ever used it had been around the time when Mother died. He had probably picked up the habit again from Eleanor.

"Jane — thee doesn't think I would ever forget thy mother, does thee? "

" No — not *forget* her, actually."

" I couldn't, thee knows. And especially not now that thee's begun sometimes to remind me of her, in the way thee looks and speaks."

He went away then, without saying anything more, the sound of his footsteps soon dying away down the path. Kai looked hopefully after him, then turned his head with an inquiring bark.

"All right, you go along, Kai." She gave him a gentle shove. Then she looked down at the pearls. They felt cool and smooth, coiled in her hand; the soft, gold sunlight made the tiny diamond initial on the locket sparkle. She stared at them for a long time.

Suddenly it seemed as if there was some mysterious new life pouring into everything around her. The familiar trees, the stones, the water, even every blade of grass, looked clear and bright, as if — as if they were lighted up and glowing from inside. If she didn't move, if she hardly breathed, it would stay like that for a while — and so would that feeling of deep comfort welling up in her heart. Why, this was it! This was what poetry was about — and love — and religion — and everything that was beautiful! This was the way things always were — if you could see them the right way. Yes, and this must be at least the beginnings of what the older Friends called an " opening " — but now the magic was fading and vanishing.

How long had the whole strange experience lasted? Jane held the pearls against her cheek — they were as warm as her hand.

She got up. Whatever it was that had happened was over. It hadn't been anything she could ever describe to anyone. But it *had* happened. It would never really be over and gone as long as she lived. The warm, soft feeling in her heart was still there.

She began to run; she ran all the way to the cottage. Her father was sitting at his desk not doing anything at all, and she suddenly felt shy. Was he going to make it hard to explain things?

" Dad — "

" Yes? "

" Could you — that is, will you call Eleanor and say would she please come and have supper with us because it's my birthday? "

He turned quickly in his chair and looked at her piercingly.

" I've just happened to — well, to change my mind. I mean, if it's all right with you. I mean about Eleanor, and as a matter of fact about Greenlands too." She took a deep breath. " I wish you'd ask Eleanor if she'd bring some extra salad greens, and a couple of tomatoes if she has any."

Her father stared at her. " You've changed your mind! Well! Far be it from me to ask any questions — "

"No, don't, Dad." Jane felt like laughing.

He reached for the telephone, still watching her cautiously. " Er — salad greens? "

Jane kissed the top of his head. " And two tomatoes! "

Chapter XVII

THERE was a rustle in the apple tree, a soft plop, and
Jane looked down in surprise at the fruit where it lay
in the grass at her feet. So the tree had borne after all,
even though it was so old and neglected. This one apple,
at least, had ripened quietly out of sight somewhere among
the leaves, and now glowed softly red in the grass. Were
there other apples up in the tree? A few months ago she
would have known everything that went on up there, but
now she stopped to remember that climbing a tree meant
getting her clothes messy, and twigs and pieces of bark in
her hair.

"Hi!" Mary Lee came out of the cottage door. "I biked
over to bring your pop a special-delivery letter."

"Hi, Mary Lee. Dad isn't home right now."

"I put it on his desk. What's that nice smell?"

"Early fall, I guess. Or wood shavings."

"When the new wing on the cottage is finished, will you
have your bedroom in it, Jane?"

"No, I'm going to keep the one I have now, but we're
going to take down a wall, and it'll be twice as big."

"Listen," said Mary Lee; "I wanted to ask you something."

"What?"

"Larry and I are going out to the Meads' tomorrow to
pick blackberries and have a picnic, the way we do every

182

year before school starts. Would you and Pete like to come along? "

" I don't know exactly."

" Well, ask him, why don't you? I've hardly even seen him since I got back from the lake."

" You didn't expect to, Mary Lee, did you? I mean, not like before? " Mary Lee did not reply. Jane, feeling her heart begin to beat faster, swallowed and went on. " We never have talked about it at all, Mary Lee — and I hope you don't mind my bringing it up now. But before that night when Larry came back from the lake, you saw Pete all the time."

" I know." Mary Lee sat down on the step and propped her chin in her hands. " I suppose Pete did get a jolt when Larry and I patched things up. Pete's very attractive, and maybe nobody ever threw him over before."

" You did encourage him, Mary Lee, and you never said anything to him about being Larry's girl."

" I know. I was swept off my feet for a while there. But, Jane, I don't think it amounted to much for either of us. He was feeling low, and there wasn't anybody around except you and me, and he thought of you as a kid. For a while I was mixed up, and I didn't want to cool Pete off by saying much of anything about Larry. I can tell you, Jane, I still feel shaky when I think how close I came to losing Larry for good. He was so mad — "

" It wasn't just Pete, was it? I mean, Larry was thinking about other times."

" Yes, but this was more serious — at least, I thought so for a little while. Jane, I know the girls at school think I'm always trying to attract a lot of boys I shouldn't. I don't think going steady is the thing for everybody, but if you do, then you shouldn't hurt the other person."

" Then why do you make Larry jealous? "

" Well — this is kind of hard to say. You see, Jane, practically all of you at Halford School have fathers who are professors and went to college and so on, and my father didn't. You know what it's like at our house — we don't have a lot of things you do — you know what I mean! You'd still be Jane Greene if you lived in a rabbit hutch — it isn't money that makes the difference. But being popular with boys helps me feel better about all that."

"Oh, Mary Lee! I didn't know you felt like that! And it's so silly."

"I know it is. I never told anyone before. Maybe that was one reason I latched onto Pete, though. I was impressed because he was from New York and went to prep school and so on. You see him a lot nowadays, don't you?"

Jane felt uncomfortable. "Sure I do, but then I have all along. We're cousins and all — "

"Personally, I think you have dates with him!" said Mary Lee.

"Not like — not like real dates. Of course, I don't know anything about real dates unless you could count going out with Mario — and he wasn't here very long."

Mary Lee laughed. "He was here long enough for Pete to notice that Mario fell for you like a ton of bricks. Anyhow, if it isn't real dates with Pete, I predict it soon will be. I like those Bermuda shorts on you, Jane, and that coral lipstick. I'd better get back to Halford, but you remember what I said. So long, Jane — Hello, Julian Greene!" Jane's father came from the cottage, a letter in his hand.

"So long, Mary Lee." Jane slipped her arm through her father's. "I came out to look at the new wing before the men come, and got talking to Mary Lee."

"It doesn't look like much but a pile of bricks and lumber yet. I tried to get the foreman to tell me yesterday before they knocked off when he thought they'd be done, but he was very cagey and wouldn't commit himself."

"They'd better not be too long, or Eleanor will go out

of her mind; she wants to start decorating. I'm going to Maryville with her tomorrow to look at wallpapers, and if we can't find any we like there, we'll have to go to Columbus. She's hatching some scheme about my room too; I suspect she's going to want something with daisies all over it, but I can handle that."

"I have the official letter from the trustees with the final offer for Greenlands."

"Oh, is that the letter Mary Lee brought?"

"No." He looked a little confused. "That's something else again. The letter about Greenlands came yesterday, but I've been waiting for a good chance to tell you about it. I didn't want to bring it up with the Greenes all here yesterday evening —"

"Oh." How nervously poor Dad was looking at her! No wonder, after what he'd been through all summer with her fussing. "I'm glad you heard from them. Is it O.K.? Enough money, I mean, and all settled and everything?"

"Yes, they met my figure, and it's more than enough for our needs. It'll clear our debts and pay for the addition to the cottage. Of course, we're actually buying the cottage and its grounds out of the Greenlands estate. I said we'd have to have four acres around it. That'll give us room to garden! We'd better start thinking about perennials. And the acreage includes that clump of sycamores you're fond of."

"I never even knew you knew I liked those trees."

"And a college fund for you. Oh, we're very prosperous! You'll be able to go anywhere you like, though, of course, Eleanor and I hope you'll want to stay at Halford. The money takes the pressure off all around."

"I think it's wonderful. I could go to one of the American Friends Service Committee work camps next summer."

"Would you like to?"

" Maybe. Pete's been thinking he might do that."

" Oh? "

" He's been talking about it some, off and on." Heavens, Dad was looking at her almost coyly! " Uncle Charles would like him to. You like having Pete's father back from Europe, don't you? "

" Yes. I've stopped moping since Charles came — about the presidency, I mean, and the house too. He's exactly the man the college needs. I'm going over to play chess with him at Greenlands tonight. Listen, Jane — "

" What? " His tone had changed, and now he sat down on the step and looked at her.

" Do you feel ready for another piece of important news? This special delivery is from Jean. She says she's made up her mind about something I knew she was considering, but still I'm rather bowled over. You know, there's always been this particular problem between Jean and me about money. I've never been willing to accept any from her for you or me or your mother's medical bills or for Greenlands."

" I know, Dad — because it's war-profit money. I guess you're right, but it has hurt Jean's feelings."

" I know, and I'm sure I could have at least have been more tactful in the way I refused. Well, this is Jean's present idea. Halford has never had enough facilities for a good art department, because Quakers were still rather suspicious of art in the days when it was founded. Jean wants to give the college an art building; it would be a combination of a little museum, crafts rooms, pottery, studio rooms, and so on. It would be named for your mother as a memorial to her. It's very generous of Jean. In her will, she plans to leave the rest of her money to found some art scholarships and perhaps to add a little theater to the building, again in your mother's name. But

186

she doesn't want to do it, she says, unless we both approve."

"Oh, Dad, I do! I approve completely, don't you? I think it's wonderful! "

"Are you sure? It's an important decision. You're pretty certain to come in for a portion at least of Jean's property one day, in spite of anything she says when she's in a temper with me, and you might be sorry if you decide in a hurry. I'm a little tired of hearing how ' impractical ' I am. If I influence you to give up the chance of one day having a very solid income — "

"Oh, Dad, stop talking like that, please, because I don't need to think it over. Tell Jean I think it's a sensationally wonderful idea. Couldn't we take Mother's paintings from Greenlands and have them together in a room in the new building? You said they should be displayed as a collection."

"We could. I thought of it too. And you and I and Eleanor could pay for building that room as our contribution. Well, then, Jane — you really are determined to give up your chance to be an heiress? "

"Oh, heiresses! I've got everything I want — almost. If I can pass my algebra make-up when school starts next week — "

"Pete says you're sure to. Is that a car coming up the drive? "

"Yes, and it isn't the convertible either, or Eleanor's car, or Hanson's truck. I know all their engines. Let's go see."

"Hey, Jane! " The old car from the barn rattled into sight as they came out the front door. It stopped with a shudder, and Pete leaped out of it. "We did it! She isn't tamed yet, but she's running! And you were kidding me last week because I took out a license for her! Come on, hop in. The twins were yelling for a ride, but I said you had to be the first passenger."

" Oh, Pete! But I haven't even done the breakfast dishes."

" Take her along, Pete." Dad opened the door for her. Kai at once leaped into the back seat as if he had been riding in that car all his life.

They shot down the drive. " I'll have to adjust the engine so it won't make such a racket," Pete shouted. " I think I know how."

" I just thought of something! You can't take the car to school with you. The students don't have cars there — you told me."

" Can't hear you!" Pete turned into Halford Road. " Let's go show the car to Wilbur Baker."

" I said, you can't take the car to school with you! "

" It's all right; I'm not going back there."

" Stop! Stop the car this minute, Pete Greene! I'm not going to yell like this! "

" Oh, all right." He pulled up under the shade of a trailing willow.

" Pete " — Jane felt a cold chill of fear — " what do you mean about school? Aren't you all right after all? Aunt Marion said Dr. Jerome said you could go."

" Sure, I'm all right; don't get excited. I've decided to stay at Halford for my senior year, that's all. I might even end up going to college here; who knows? " he added sulkily. " Though all I can say is, I hope Dad's got a halfway decent science department here by then."

" But — but what's it all about? All summer you've been talking about going back east to school and how terrible it would be if you couldn't."

" People change their minds."

" Sure they do, but, Pete — why did you, about this? Is it — is it maybe that if you stayed around, Mary Lee might — might change her mind about Larry? "

" Mary Lee! Whatever gave you that notion? I should say not! That was all very nice while it lasted, and I'm not sore at her any more, though I was for a while. But no girl gets a chance to throw me over twice. No; the thing is, I couldn't figure out when I thought it over who was going to look after you, if I didn't stick around to do it. You're so mixed up; you'll probably be in a jam in no time at all. Having fights with poor old Eleanor, probably — "

" I will not have fights with Eleanor! That's awfully mean to say, Pete, and completely unfair! I get along perfectly well with Eleanor now! "

Pete began to laugh. " That's another reason somebody has to look after you — or you'll never have any sense of humor at all."

" I have too. I think lots of things are funny now, that I never used to think were." She didn't know if her voice sounded convincingly angry or not — because underneath being a little bit angry at the things Pete was saying was another kind of feeling, a shaky feeling.

" Now I'll tell you one thing I don't think is funny," said Pete, " and that's Mario writing you letters. That isn't a real riot."

" Oh! How did you know? "

" Mary Lee told me. She sees them at the post office."

" Oh."

" Also, when we went to the movies last night you tried to pay for your own ticket. I was taking you out. *Also,* when you opened your bag I spotted a letter from Mario in it. Now we'll have no more of that."

" You — you're taking an awful lot for granted, Pete."

" Am I? Am I, Jane? " Now he was looking at her quite seriously.

" I still — well, I still think — you and Mary Lee — "

" That never did amount to much, and anyway, Mary Lee is neither here nor there. It never would have amounted to anything, even if she hadn't turned me down for Larry."

"I don't see how she could—" Jane stopped. What a giveaway kind of thing to have said! And she had always been so careful! It must be due to feeling terribly rattled by the things Pete had been saying.

He smiled. "It seemed peculiar to me too!"

"Naturally," said Jane, talking rapidly, "I don't *mind* if you stay in Halford, because Aunt Marion will be glad. But it's silly for you to say you have to look after me or anything like that."

"I wouldn't be too terribly surprised," said Pete calmly, "if some distant day this whole thing turned into one of these Greene cousin deals — maybe by the time I'm president of Halford myself. Now, I'm not guaranteeing a thing, of course," he added warningly. "But say it should happen to work out that way — someday — why then, Jessica Jane Greene, thee'd get thyself back into Greenlands that way."

"I don't — I never —" Jane sputtered.

"Thee's such an obstinate type —"

"I haven't said — I haven't said —"

"Thee doesn't need to say anything. I'm glad thee's managed to turn thyself into a girl this summer, but be sure thee keeps on trying to improve thyself. Did thee wash behind thy ears today?"

"Pete!"

He yanked her over to him, too suddenly for resistance, even if she had tried. He kissed her quickly and started up the car again.

"Pete! Pete! I just remembered something! There's a rosebud tea set in the coal cellar at Greenlands!"

"Is there? Well, fine!"

And as the car leaped jerkily forward along the dusty, sunny road, they were both laughing.

Biography of Edith Spacil Gilmore

EDITH SPACIL GILMORE grew up in Newburyport, Massachusetts, a town with a tendency to produce writers. She was graduated from Radcliffe College, where she tumbled more or less accidentally into the field of Germanic Languages and Literature and liked it. She kept on with the academic life and took a Ph.D. in Germanics at Yale, with a couple of years off for teaching at Windsor Mountain School and the University of California. She married Robert Wallace Gilmore, a psychologist, in 1948. They went on a bicycle youth hostel trip in Europe and through it they became familiar with the work of the American Friends Service Committee abroad. This led to an increasing interest in the Quakers, to Quaker-directed volunteer work, chiefly with young people, to membership in a Friends Meeting, and at last, on Robert Gilmore's part, to full-time work for the American Friends Service Committee as head of its New York office. Edith Gilmore also left teaching, as her interest in creative writing and various kinds of volunteer work increased. She has published translations of works in German, and has written for *Seventeen* and other periodicals.

The Gilmores have a microscopic New York apartment and a smallish country cottage which contains two Siamese cats and a hi-fi outfit that is usually playing baroque music.